1994 Supportive Community

FLOATING CANDLES

FLOATING CANDLES

by

Mari Shimasaki

A Hearthstone Book

Carlton Press, Inc.   New York, N.Y.

DEDICATION

The compilation of *Floating Candles* is dedicated to our four children, Margo, Mark, Kent and Kevin, who have given us fulfillment, meaning, and richness to our lives.

May the vast experience of how we all fitted into the global societies of the world continue to give direction, creativity, sense of values, and moral integrity.

May your exposure not only to the supportive community of your family and friends, but also to the poverty, want and the maimed, to the imbalance between the haves and the have-nots find expressions through your sensitivity and actions as you journey through life.

FLOATING CANDLES

Amman, Jordan
Christmas, 1959

At the crossroads of life, Bill and I had been reassessing our lives, values, and purpose of life, when an opportunity opened for Bill with Harza Engineering Co. of Chicago for the East Ghor Irrigation Project in the Jordan Valley. To have a hand in making the desert bloom, the dream of 2.000 years? And in the Holy Land?

We gave up our beautiful home and comfortable life in the Columbia Basin, enplaned in Seattle in late October for Jordan via London with Margo 6, Mark 4, and Kent 9 months old. Mysterious vistas opened as we winged our way, soaring above the abyss of the universe. We had our first glimpse of the blue Mediterranean coastline, and handsome Beirut, and flew on to Amman, Jordan in a prop plane.

At the Continental Hotel, our first class VIP treatment was over, and we were esconced in two rooms on two floors in downtown Amman, the capital city. At 6:00 a.m. we were suddenly awakened to the blasting call from outside our window. It was a muezzin in the minaret of a mosque, calling the faithful to prayers. We were, indeed, in a Moslem country!

Bill took an early walk around the block and returned to report that four bodies, victims of political intrigue, were hanging in the public square behind our hotel. After Bill left to attend an orientation to his work in the Jordan Valley, I followed careful instructions from our friend and with uneasy feelings put Margo into a taxi with specific instructions to the driver to take her to the American School, as I was tied down with two exhausted and sleeping boys. We had all visited the school the day before and Margo had met the principal and teachers. The Arabs love children and ours made a big hit with them. Margo and Mark are picking up greetings and phrases faster than we are.

The director of the American Friends of the Middle East, Rev. and Mrs. Hulac were gracious and offered the use of their spacious home located next door to the American School, while they were away. Getting acquainted with a temperamental geezer, a water heater that either literally gorged up oiled bags of packed sawdust or stubbornly refused even a little smoke, was a frustrating experience to me, indeed. Houses have no central heat, the terrazo floors are ice cold and Amman is 4,000 ft. in elevation. The children all have sniffles.

From the grocer who came to the house daily on a bicycle, I ordered, with difficulty, what I thought was a Thanksgiving turkey. What actually turned up was a fragile, pin-feathered tubercular specimen of a chicken. I was heartsick! Drinking water must be boiled to a hard rolling boil for 20 minutes. Sterilizing vegetables was a disaster, as I was told to use a detergent. Unfortunately, the vegetable was cauliflower. Cold water, granules of Tide and crevasses in the vegetable! I soaked it too long and the cauliflower came out pink. As we sat down to Thanksgiving dinner, I admit we didn't feel particularly thankful.

Within a few weeks, we found a three bedroom furnished duplex and quickly settled in. I had traded my automatic clothes washer for a Spin Dry, but our ship freight won't arrive for five months. Happily, the Hulacs sent a friend of their cook, and Jacob proved to be a real Godsend. A Palestinian refugee, he had never worked in a home and I had never had help in our home, but Jacob, who speaks Arabic French and English, was a marvel and we divided our work. He insisted on doing the handwash, but my Oriental background would not permit a man to do such menial work, and so I commenced my mornings on my knees at the bathtub with the diapers, etc. It gave me time to ponder on all the things for which I was thankful. What a time of soul searching, living in a country where poverty seemed to be a way of life for so many.

Just before Christmas came a frantic call for volunteers at the newly organized Boy's Club. "Would you come and help with favors, decorations, goodies?" Since I had wonderful Jacob to babysit after I put the children to bed, I went to help and was introduced to shoeless, almost clothesless boys, age 5-15, 150 in all—all refugees. The club is headed by a tireless Arab, Yousef, who works with the help and donations from the American community. What a happy occasion when each boy was given a suit of clothes, shoes and socks for his first Christmas. We taught them games and happy Christmas carols. I am already involved in putting together a children's pageant for the English speaking Sunday School group that meets at the American Embassy.

The first joyous Christmas tidings went out from a place so close by; the significance of Jerusalem and Bethlehem leaves me devoid of human expressions. We miss you and love you all. Bill's work in the tropical Jordan Valley has really stepped up and we see him only on Wednesday night, and Saturday noon to Sunday. Kent loves his stroller on wheels, and we can keep this active dynamo off of the cold tile floor for only part of the time. Margo, Mark, Kent join us in singing with you *In Excelsis Deo.*

Amman, Jordan
Christmas, 1960

Greetings from the Holy Land! Already we have lived through a kaleidscope of events and highlights among a people and a culture we have learned to admire and to love.

Jordan was the only Arab country that had welcomed the refugees from Palestine during the 1948 war. This poor country, bereft of fertile land, water, and resources, except for potash, is harboring today a refugee population that constitutes

11

one-third of the total population. We visited the largest refugee camp near Jericho and the Mt. of Temptation. The camp is juxtaposed to the barren and craggy wilderness of Judea. Amman is bulging within, and in the suburbs, with refugees. Caves are standard places of abodes for many. Many of the well educated and wealthy Palestinians have opened schools, stores, companies and banks. We are in the midst of a four year drought and UNRWA (United Nations Rehabilitation Works Agency) trucks are delivering water to isolated villages, one gallon per family per day, and theirs is an extended family. We, too, hardly go a week when water is not turned off for several hours or days. The refugee camps are dens of discontent, breeding grounds for violence, frustrations, poverty; festering under constant bombardment of tirades and propaganda.

We have met Miss Husseini, relative of one of the top engineers who works with Bill. She opened her home to over a hundred children who flooded into the old city of Jerusalem during the first few days of fighting. The home has been expanded into a school as well. Miss Halaby, who had been an underground guerilla fighter, has started a school and "artisannat," a handcraft center for girls. The center is now famous for its embroidery and quality of work. We are also in touch with the Haramy brothers, one is a principal of boy's school in Ramallah and the other is head of the UNRWA Vocational School in Amman. They are related to Dr. Haramy, a physician of Winona Lake, Indiana, whom I met at the lake.

Bill's work is picking up momentum and he is very enthusiastic. They have employed nearly 2,000 refugees to hand dig the main canal in order to give employment to those who are desperately in need. Many men look across the Jordan River and see their land, orchard, and homes as grim reminders of injustices. What is the meaning, the logic, of making a home for displaced persons, only to displace others? Bill's field office is located on Tel Dier Allah, which is Succoth in the Bible. Succoth is the place where Esau and Jacob had their reconciliation.

Through the cooperation of the Ministry of Social Welfare and the U.S. Gov't. Wives Club, the Amman Baby Home has been started. It is staffed by Jordanian women and volunteer American and Jordanian wives. We have learned about swaddling clothes, and homemade rice and vegetable purees. Love is a universal language and the babies respond to the cuddling and talking to. Some were found under bushes in the desert or left on doorsteps, or just abandoned.

The Bible becomes more alive as we visit the old city, the Dead Sea, Jericho, Nablus, Ramallah, Samaria and Jacob's Well. Everywhere are the cripples, deformed, the sightless, the emaciated—eyes and faces so beautiful, which speak so much. My 80-yr, old mother is visiting us and she whispered in compassion, "If Jesus were here, they could be healed."

We've gotten used to the geezer, the portable kerosene stoves in the bedrooms, eating prickly cactus fruits, and now are able to communicate somewhat in Arabic. A Vokswagen Bug helps us get around. Mark and Margo have transferred to the British School and are getting a good start in their academic life under Headmistress Miss Webster. "The Atomic Kid" is Kent's nickname, as he has learned to walk, go up and down steps, climb pianos, chairs, tables, and windows. He's learning to speak in Arabic, English, and Japanese, the latter thanks to my mom. She was so thrilled to be in the Holy Land and, while here, has again read the entire Bible in Japanese. Having walked where Jesus walked, ministered and died has been so wonderful that she says, she is ready for death at any time.

What a thrill to be in Bethlehem on Christmas Eve and then to participate in the service at Shepherd's Field, as we watched for the first star to appear over the city of Bethlehem. As the angels proclaimed that night, *"Glory To God In The Highest And On Earth Peace Goodwill Towards Men"* may this Message of Peace ring throughout the world. And so in Arabic we say, Aiid Milad

Jordan—Palestinian refugees lining the canal on the East Ghor Canal Project

Madison, Wisconsin
Christmas, 1961

Winging our way from Jordan to Wisconsin, we bring you our greetings and fresh memories of our rich experiences in the Holy Land. We feel humble to be able to share the inspiration of having walked His paths, His fields, gazed at His Heavens. The crippled, blind, sick still endure; the tents, shepherds and sheep are still to be seen; the stark nakedness of the barren hills and the relentless heat of summer are still to be borne; and the struggles of the refugees remain a grim reminder of the early Christian refugees who fled from Jerusalem to the hills of Pella. The aged and gnarled olive trees in the Garden of Gethsemane still bend the knees and hearts of those who gaze upon them.

Life in Jordan?

Margo: "I think it's terrible how in America they let the drinking fountains run all day long. Don't they know Jordan and other places need that water?" Mark in London, "Hey, Margo, this is real cow's milk!" Kent during play, "This is Rome, this is London, Beirut, and Aqaba." Margo, "I'll probably open Auntie Mae's refrigerator when I want a drink of water and then I'll feel really silly." (In Jordan water is boiled and cooled in the refrigerator.) Mark, "Hey T.V. and milk shakes! Real neat!" Mary, "Now children this is America. There's plenty of hot water, fill up the tub."

The children and I arrived in Madison, last of September, via Rome and London, to get reacquainted with part of our family, to be reoriented to American society, and to await the arrival of our new addition. Bill joins us in December and then in January, we return to Jordan where Bill's work still remains.

Margo, 8, allayed everyone's apprehension when she remarked after her first peek at her third brother. "Why he looks just like Baby Jesus!" She's a voracious reader, avid collector of artifacts, stamps, rocks, shells, and virtually eats school.

Mark, 6. His mode of walking is not on two feet, but rather

15

Margo

Mark

Kent

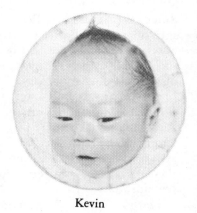

Kevin

rolling, cavorting over expanses of American lawns. He worships his ten-yr. old cousin and is getting pointers in football.

Kent, 2. Don't let the angelic pose fool you! But he does have his winsome ways. An all-round outgoing, friendly character, he's joined a family of swimmers, diving and floating at age two

Kevin William, born Nov. 8, poses at age 30 hrs. and is already airborne.

We're proud of Bill for the challenge he feels in his works. The company just completed the first of three stages of the East Ghor Irrigation Canal in the Jordan Valley. He is dedicated and works against elements of weather, outdated working methods, frustrations, and red tape. It was a rare thrill when we witnessed the first water filling the laterals in what appeared an impossible and unyielding desert. Mary kept busy with family, Arabic studies, part-time student counseling for Jordanians at the American Friends of the Middle East, summer fun time activities for Mark's age group, and serving on the steering committee for the International English speaking Sunday services. Entering this glad season threatened with talk of bomb shelters and international tensions, may we say in Arabic *Merry Christmas*.

Jerusalem, 1962

I am writing to you from the roof of the Old Gloria Hotel in the heart of the old quarters in Jerusalem. It is 6:00 in the morning and I am anxious to share with you something of what I see, hear, and feel. I am caught in this overwhelming milieu, the call to prayer from the minaret of the mosque and the cacaphony of clarion tolls from the belfry of the cathedrals of the Roman Catholic, Russian Orthodox, Coptic, and Armenian churches. This holy city truly sings its exhilaration and its laments of today as it has in bygone days. Something intangible and ethereal in the spirit is here, and no one can escape it.

I stand in awe with all my senses honed sharp. Verses from the Bible flow through me, "But seek ye first the Kingdom of God...Love thy Lord thy God with all your heart, and mind, and soul...and thy neighbor as thyself."

Bill has joined me and he is pointing to the Gold Dome of the Mosque of Omar, the El Aksa Mosque, the Church of the Sepulchre and the Gate of Hadrian, which leads into the remains of the grounds of Solomon's Temple. We are trying to get our bearings—Damascus Gate, St. Stephen's Gate, Dung Gate and where is the Garden Tomb?

I look down on the cobblestone streets that etch a maze of winding paths. They speak to me of the events in the synagogue, the visit to the temple, the money changers, the stoning of Stephen, the Stations of the Cross. The white or gray-plastered houses, apartments, shops, cafes line the streets like huddled gossipy women. We see donkeys laden with wares being carried toward the souks, markets. Bedouin girl, dressed in black, embroidered gowns, deftly balance jugs or cans on their heads. They make their way towards the watering places. Arab children, dressed in their royal blue smocks, dart in and out playing tag, their school bags flying. Two old men in flowing, brown galabiyas and wearing red fezzes on their heads are gesticulating as they turn a corner. A young man in a Western gray suit strides along carrying his briefcase. His head is covered with the red and white Arab kaffia (scarf) held down with black head rings. A beggar in rags shuffles along, stopping to peer into the garbage drums, while an elderly man dressed in traditional clothes moves along, carrying his hubbly-bubbly water pipe, as he makes his way to find his place among his old cronies outside Damascus Gate.

Over to our right is Mandlebaum Gate, just a stone's throw from us, and we can see the guards, rifles in hands, on the wall. The gate is the point of no return that divides Israel from Jordan. I can distinguish the YMCA and the rooftops of

18

the new Jerusalem on the Israeli side. The Wailing Wall that covers some of the original stones from the Temple of Solomon is forbidden to the Jews.

Listening to the heartbeat of this sacred city, we are convinced that this is a holy city and should be internationalized, a city open to all faiths. It is near the birthplace of Jesus, harbors the ties with Abraham, Haggar and Ishmael for the Moslems, and Abraham, Sarah and Isaac for the Jews and Protestants. Jerusalem is rooted in the sacred, the holy, the heart of the Holy Land.

And once again Jesus wept, "O Jerusalem, Jerusalem, you who kill the prophets and stone those sent to you; how often I have longed to gather your children together, as a hen gathers her young under his wings, but you were not willing."

At this season, let us remember to live by, *"Love The Lord Your God With All Your heart, With all Your Soul And With All Your Mind. Love Your Neighbor As Yourself...Judge Not that you Be Judged."*

What a thrill when Bill and colleagues received the highest civilian gold medal from King Hussein for their work with the East Ghor Canal and Irrigation Project. Bill says he had a wonderful crew of Jordanian engineers. We are truly proud of Bill's work as Field Engineer of this construction. The final blasting was completed in building the tunnel, which brought the water from the Yarmouk River, located between Syria and Jordan, into the main canal. We all virtually wept when we witnessed the opening of the main gate that brought the first waters into the irrigation system. Our special guest Mrs. Rodeheaver was a witness at this great event with King Hussein, government officials, family, etc.

The children are all thriving in school and in their many activities. I am having a ball teaching two hours, twice a week, at the Ahliyyah Girls's School, a private girl's elementary and high school. Princess Basman is a student here. She is given no special privileges, and she shivers in the unheated school in winter with all of us. Most of the girls I teach are preparing for the General Certificate of Education, British equivalent to our College Boards, but much more comprehensive. Love from all of us to you.

Arlington Heights, Illinois
Christmas, 1963

The family is gathered around the hearth in this very comfortable family room. The letter of a year ago written from Jerusalem and Christmas in Bethlehem all seem like fantasies already, but experiences to be cherished forever.

The activities so varied and experiences so abundant, all squeezed into a single year, seem incredulous. During the Ramadan Holiday in February, we took Margo and Mark on a quick trip to Cairo and Athens. In May Bill wound up Harza's construction of the East Ghor Canal Project, having a hand in putting 100,000 acres under irrigation in the Jordan Valley. Then a round of reluctant and tearful farewells and departure from Beirut aboard the "Esperia" for Naples via Alexandria and Sicily; the picturesque Bay of Sorrento; World War II landmarks of the Japanese-American 442 combat team; majestic Mt. Vesuvius and Pompeii...life snuffed out in an instant...could history repeat itself? The motor trip from Naples by the magnificent Tyrrhenian coastline to Rome; a night at a tucked-away villa near Sienna, associated with Garibaldi; the straw market in Florence and Italian masterpieces; the awe-inspiring "David" by Michaelangelo; several nights at a converted Medici Palace; and the University of Padua, remembering Galileo, Dante, and Boccaccio, which left us infused with the aura of the medieval and church history.

Enchanting Venice with its street cafes and concerts under the stars in the magnificent St. Marks Square; children more occupied with pigeons and comparing different types of toilets rather than imbibing the magnificent architecture and art; on through lush, lush valleys, up the winding roads through the Italian Alps; delightful pastoral scenes; exchanging charades with friendly Austrians, breath-taking Grossglockner Pass; chair lift over the Tyrols; picnics beside clear and raging rivers; and sleeping in feather beds. We shopped in the rain in Zurich and Lucerne; drank in the serenity of the Black Forest; then raced along the autobahn, which jealousy guarded us from a view of the Rhine; on to Amsterdam and Anne Frank's hide-out—another scar left in the field of human relations; canal trips; children's miniature village outside the Hague; climbing three flights of stairs straight up to our rooms in a charming Dutch pension; and a quick hop by jet to home.

So we have settled into suburban life, Bill joining the ranks of commuters into Chicago, except for a two month detail to Nicaragua for the company. Margo, 10 1/2, has adjusted well from a small British school to a Jr. High sixther with an enrollment of 3,000. Mark, 8 1/2, rides his bike, weather permitting; instead of going to school by taxi. Kent, 4 1/2, underwent eye surgery and now is back to his normal, bump-tuous routine, and Kevin, 2, is trying to keep up with all his seniors and gets an "A" for effort.

What the New Year may bring, we do not know, but we are thankful for the bountiful blessings of this year and our heartfelt wishes go to each of you with these words of Micah:

"And he shall stand and shall feed his flock
in the strength of the Lord...and this man
shall be our *Peace*.

Conakry, Guinea, West Africa—1964

The palm fronds swaying in the ocean breeze, the fragrance of bougainvillea, the hot and humid climate of the tropics six degrees from the equator all seem like anachronism to the traditional white Christmas.

We think of all our friends scattered around the globe and bring you greetings from the capital city of Conakry, Republic of Guinea, West Africa. Our Christmas season will be shared with the American personnel, the native Christians, various African Embassy representatives, and some of the medical team and workers on board the Hospital Ship "Hope," which docked in Conakry on October 15, just before our arrival. I am in the midst of organizing a children's choir for our Protestant mission. We shall present a simple Christmas tableau under the stars by the ocean. One carol will be sung in French, and a Nigerian angel will be in the nativity scene. In a country where the people are 85% Moslems, telling the Christmas story will be a challenge.

The adjustments have been great and numerous, including climatic change, enrolling Margo, Mark, and Kent in the just-established American School where Margo is the only 7th grader. Kent has had only one semester of Kindergarten, but the principal wanted him in the first grade.

I haggle over vegetables and fish on the front porch or in the native markets, buy yard-long delicious French bread daily from the local bakery, enjoy watching the supple movements of women attired in their vivid-colored sarong-like skirts and overblouses as they balance large pans or trays of bananas, pineapples, or wood on their heads while carrying an adorable baby strapped to their backs. We have no telephone, and all take a weekly dosage of malaria pills. The dimmed lights in the evening due to lack of current are all part of our life now. We enjoy the friendly laughter and greeting of, "C'est va bien? by children as we drive or walk down the winding roads lined with plastered houses or picturesque round, thatched-roofed paillots.

Our house is a large, plastered, concrete-block, four-bedroom house with tile floors and corrugated metal roof. We are close to the ocean and we have neighbors living in paillots; the windows have no glass, only louvered shutters. The screens we have added throughout the house are a great luxury and comfort, and now we sleep with all the windows wide open with a night guard posted outside.

The children are busy with school, numerous parties involving American and embassy families, and swimming lessons taught by a Peace Corps wife. Margo is happy to have part-time use of the foot-pump organ belonging to the Protestant Mission. Little Kevin, who just turned three, has enrolled in the French Nursery School and will leave us all trailing behind in our language pursuits. French, the official spoken language is absolutely a requisite here.

Bill leaves Thursday for the eight-hour drive to Sierra Leone through the jungles to bring back materials and equipment for his work as the engineer for the USAID Mission here. I am confident he can cope with the terrible roads, no motels, no gas stations nor garages, and no restaurants. We are enjoying, however, the family-togetherness after his trips to Nicaragua, Holland, and Turkey during the past year.

As soon as our Peugeot station wagon arrives from France, supposedly today, and our boat from the States arrive, we shall be taking trips into the bush and regular trips to the sand-covered island for swimming and fishing. You might be interested to know there is no grocery store, drug store, park, library, etc. One Bata Shoe store shows two pairs of shoes in the window.

Our thoughts will be with all of you as we worship Christmas Eve under the stars by the ocean, and we shall remember that the stars that shone so long ago on that first Christmas night will be the same stars watching over Jordan, America and throughout the world. God bless you and *Bon Nöel!*

Conakry, Guinea
Christmas, 1965

The crackling of thunder, streaks of lightning, and torrents of rain clattering on corrugated tin roofs are over. All is quiet and serene again with the bright sunshine to greet us each morning, the quaint native sailboats are gliding by, and at night the plenary harvest moon sends shimmering streaks across the tranquil sea as phosphorescent glimmers dance about. Is it possible we've been in Africa over a year? All the newness of malaria pills, the bouts with mosquitoes, ants, the nightly beat of African drums, sans telephone, sans musicales, sans window panes, harvesting our own papayas, bananas, and Hawaiian corn have become mundane.

Bill travels throughout the country as he has several projects scattered over a wide area. His work consists of rehabilitation of existing riceland projects that were originally constructed by the French, prior to the Guinean independence. Rehabilitation involves repairing structures, dikes and canals. One such project of almost 4,000 acres was completed during the last year, increasing production from two to three-fold. Other projects are to be repaired and put into full production during the coming dry season in November-June. There is an annual shortage of 5,000 tons of rice each year, so this work is important. Bill is primarily a field man, and happiest when he can be out where the work is done.

Our schedules include helping new families who arrive with no housing prospects, entertaining lonesome Peace Corps volunteers and wife-less husbands, serving on the School Board and substitute teaching, Girl Scouts, daily French lessons, supervising children's activities and homework, Sunday School, social and business entertainment, a brief hop by air to Freetown to shop for a much-need windshield, and zooming out to the idyllic isle for swimming and waterskiing.

As an interlude, we enjoyed a family excursion last April into the interior where using our car heater was a unique experience. We viewed the great Kinkon waterfalls, slept near termite-infested door in the only hotel available, woke up to a fog-enshrouded morning, which slowly unveiled a spectacular panorama of lush verdure. For Easter vacation, we took the seven-hour drive by car through dusty and rugged roads and crossed two rivers on tugboat ferries to Sierra Leone for a shopping spree. We attended the Wesley Methodist Church and were thrilled at the marvelous choir. We shall never forget the cordiality of the congregation nor the white-gloved ushers dressed in formal tails.

We took a flight in August to the Canary Islands (unfortunately Bill was too busy) for three and a half weeks of much needed rest and change. We enjoyed the apartment by La Plage de Las Canteras and the much-missed amenities of life, dining out, dance typico Canario, zoo, Christopher Columbus Museum, and buying candy and ice cream.

Friends from USIS and I organized a trip last June for the American School children to go on an overnight trip to the village of Boffa on the Rio Pongo. The principal couldn't bear leaving any of the children, so we took them all, accompanied by a Hope Ship nurse. We were moved by the remains of a slave prison, the last jumping off place for points abroad, and an early Portuguese trading post. A performance of "Dance Folklorique des Masques" was quite an experience. The highlight was a personally conducted tour of a typical native school and village by school children to see all facets of native life, which gave our students a chance to press oil, beat clothes against rocks, pound rice, pull manioc roots, try native toothbrushes and go into paillotes. The enthusiastic and cordial hospitality of this children to children contact undoubtedly will remain a memorable one to old and young alike.

How we miss our work with Hope Ship, but the newly organized Women's Society of Conakry has taken on much of the office and translation work. I wish you could have seen the crowds of people at the dock, well and ailing alike together with those of us who had the privilege of working with them, to bid farewell. The Hospital Ship was at Conakry for ten months and how we admire all the doctors, surgeons, specialists who gave of their time voluntarily to administer aid and to perform all kinds of surgery on the ship from brain surgery, to complicated heart, tumor surgeries, amputations, etc. The word got out about the miracles and people came in droves, some on stretchers that were carried for miles from the interior. How we all hated to see them go and our admiration go out to them.

Yesterday, the fabulous International Fashion Show, the first in Conakry, was a tremendous money-making success. The profits were used for social and medical services. The event was held on the spacious grounds of our Deputy Chief of Mission. The Russian, Hungarian, and Yugoslavian Embassies were represented in the beautiful doll display. Swaying palm trees, flowering hibiscus and hydrangeas reflected scenes in the pool. The glistening ocean, fragrance of frangipani, soft zephirs and green lawn added to the setting. Being a very cosmopolitan city, a great many countries were represented; costumes were exquisite. It was a proud mama who watched her near teenage daughter model the Japanese kimono while carrying a parosol.

Our Christmas play for the church will use the Around the World theme. We shall be combining efforts with the Guinean Protestant Church this year. Toma, Sousou, Malenki, English and French languages will be used to tell the familiar Christmas story.

We miss all of you and enjoy your letters. We are grateful to all who have so graciously made copies of our letters and mailed them out. It's time to wish you the season's greetings and to thank you all for your continued friendship. God bless you and *Bonne Année*.

Conakry, Guinea
Christmas, 1966

How we love our new home by the sea! dancing waves, luminous with glimmering phosphorescence, the reddened sky at dawn, the majestic palm trees standing like sentinels silhouetted against the moonlight night, the pounding surfs on a stormy night, and Mark's enviable patience as he fishes from the rocks in Guinean fashion—all these bits of refreshments are relished from our terrace or on the sea wall.

As a contrast to this tranquility, we remain indoors today, for guards are posted in front of all American homes. Nineteen Guineans, including the Minister of Foreign Affairs, were arrested in Ghana en route to the Organization of African States meeting in Addis Ababa. The Americans are implicated only because the passengers used an American transport, Pan-American.

Bill and I have eagerly taken this, or these days to catch up on the numerous items which have lain dormant on our agenda. First of all, the Christmas letter. The highlights of one year include a trip to Wonsan last spring, one of Bill's riceland reclamation projects in the interior. When Bill came home one day and reported the chief of this village had offered the use of his fourth wife's paillot, I thought it was time to check into things. Margo and Mark were invited to stay with our good friends, the Nigerian ambassador and their children, and we took Kent and Kevin with us for ten days of life Guinean, living in an open shed in a native village, cooking outdoors on a Guinean charcoal stove, pounding founyou with the women. Founyou is a kind of millet the people eat with hot sauce. When it is cooked it looks very much like cream of wheat. We exchanged some of their founyou with the chow mien I was preparing. I'm sure it was the first time that founyou was eaten with soy sauce and chow mien with African piri piri hot sauce.

Margo, thirteen, was graduated with honors from the eighth grade and since Conakry does not have a Jr. and Sr. High

School, she is attending a private school in Lausanne, Switzerland pursuing French classes in the morning and English in the afternoons. How we miss her, but, mutually, we count the days for the Christmas holidays.

In August we took our "Rest and Recuperation," I laughed at first, but, believe me, after two years in the tropics, we needed it. There were five hectic days in Paris and a month of sheer living, relaxing, family togetherness at our hide-away, a rented chalet in the mountains of Switzerland. We now know what a tune-up job is. The weeks slipped by with the boys enjoying cops and robbers in the woods and by the river with Swiss children, with numerous hikes in the country, shopping to get Margo ready for school, trips to Jungfrau, Grindevald, St. Bernard Tunnel and pass, Chamonix by car, teleferique, tele-chaise, telecabine, summer festival concerts in Montreaux, just 30 min. away, and nothing to say about avoirdupos gained.

In September we plunged into our duties for our last year in Guinea. In a weak moment, I agreed to teach full-time at the American School. It is turning out to be more of a panic than teaching. All in all, it's good to be back in teaching. All I need are about eight tentacles to keep everything at school and home under control. Having digested Kevin's forthright outburst last spring, "Well, how'd *you* like to be *my* age and have to go to the French school!" He now attends the private American kindergarten instead of the French Nursery.

Another year has passed, a year to remember friends, a year of acquiring new friends. Our thoughts are with each of you. May we ever hope and pray for the *Peace,* which forever keeps eluding mankind throughout the world. *Joyeux Noel!*

December 12, 1966

Much has happened in the last month. Pan-American and Peace Corps were ousted by the Guinean government. USAID decided to phase out. Bill has completed his two-year term, and so we are enjoying an unexpected early home leave before Bill is transferred to Tunisia. What a time we are having with our families in Madison, Wisconsin. Mae's daughter comes home from college this week, Bill from Washington D.C. our Margo from Switzerland for the holidays. The boys are delighted with school and all the Christmas activities. Thinking of all of you and wishing you the very best for the New year!!

Tunis, Tunisia
Christmas, 1967

Greetings from the last outpost fringing on the Sahara in the southwestern desert of Tunisia. We have driven down to the oasis of Nefta to spend Thanksgiving holidays. We are only 30 kilometers from the Algerian frontier. This is quite a change from the modern and cosmopolitan capital of Tunis, where life varies little from that in the states. The desert hotel built recently by the Touring Club is made of primitive bricks, lined in geometric design. The domed roofs over each room and the open-air ceiling in the lobby in local style gives the place charm and feeling. The boys were ecstatic with the donkey and camel rides through the oasis and through the streams fed by 150 artesian springs that water the date palm oasis. The hotel is located at the edge of the oasis, where the clay-sand desert stretches out in all directions, the horizon is broken only by the "chott" now filled by the recent rains, but which appears as a mirage most of the year. We freeze during the night and sleep under six layers of camel-hair blankets, but by day we can take sunbaths.

Our purchase of two "tarboukas" (drums) and a tambourine was just enough to get a couple of hotel people started, and the evening ended in a very lively and enjoyable Tunisian dance folklorique with our friends and hotel guests all entering in— the boys taking turns at the drums and all of us on the floor. This was one evening we all kept warm!

29

Margo, a young lady at 14, is attending Marymount International Girls' School in Rome this year and has just written us a glowing account of the school trip to Florence and Pisa over Thanksgiving weekened. Virtually imbibing history! Last summer, she enjoyed working with Mlle. Mimi at the Geological Museum, helping classify and arranging fossils. A visit by Diane Ermogenie of New York gave her companionship for part of the summer.

Mark, 12, in another few months will be taller than his dad and had been really wrapped up in Boy Scouts this year. Judo and guitar lessons and rocket launching give him a well-rounded discipline and pleasure. An avid snorkel fan, he leads his brothers into investigating old Phonecian and Roman ports. They look for Roman coins in caves and ruins around Carthage and look for empty shells on World War II battlegrounds around Kasserine and Cap Bon.

Kent remains the same active character at eight. An image of his dad, down to the horned-rim glasses, he's the mechanic and electrical bug. Whenever dad starts in with his tools, you can be sure Kent is right beside him. He won a Science award for his model of a Roman aqueduct and a mosaic bath. Tunisia has one of the best preserved Roman aqueducts, which used to bring water from Zagouan Mts. 75 miles away to Tunis-Carthage. Part of the system is still being used today. At the Halloween Parade, he was a sight, dressed as a mummy!

Kevin, who just turned six, is relieved to have joined his brothers at the American School. Having overcome his initial anxieties of not being able to read or write in English, he's learning all the pleasures, fun, and work of a first grader. For his Pirate Birthday Party, there was a Pirate Boat Cake, a treasure box to dig out of the ground, and a donkey ride for all the children. When the school principal presented himself with a shiner as a result of mishap with the garden gate, Kevin exclaimed, "Oh, lucky man, he really has something for 'Show and Tell'!" Affable and shy, he's still the lady's man of several years ago.

Bill is the Water Resources Utilization Engineer here. His

work is mainly in irrigation and domestic water improvement. Sleeping under mango trees and cooking over a native charcoal burner out in the bush country of Guinea has been superseded by first rate hotels to stay in during his field trips in Tunisia. School Board, and Arabic and French lessons keep him going.

Mary keeps herself busy and enjoys her volunteer work at Bir Kassa Elementary School for the Blind, working with younger children in music, games, rhythmics and dance. You should hear them sing in Arabic, French and Japanese, and they love "Go In and Out the Window" and "London Bridge," and they are tremendous in doing the Grand March. We are also cutting audio-tapes in French and Arabic for the Secondary School for the Blind in Sousse.

Our year was saddened when my mother passed away in February after 85 years of active life. How we shall cherish our unexpected four weeks visit with her last winter. At this season our thoughts and hearts go out to Jerusalem and Bethlehem, which gave us the Prince of Peace. Today that part of the world epitomizes the social ills, injustice, ideological conflicts, physical sufferings, and mental anguish felt and seen throughout the world.

"Into Thy hands, O Father, we commit our anxious and troubled world; increase our faith that in Thee and Thy son is our hope."

May we say again *Joyeux Noel!*

Tunis, Tunisia
Christmas, 1968

I am sitting on top of Byrsa Hill in Carthage and recalling the legend of Queen Dido, who left Tyre, Phoenicia, following the murder of her husband by her brother Pygmalion. After negotiating to buy a plot of land that could be encompassed

31

by a bull's hide, she cut the hide into thin strips, pieced them together. The result was the acquisition of Byrsa Hill and Dido became Queen of Carthage.

A Tunisian woman dressed in her white safsari robe is ambling down the dirt path, an Air France plane is just coming in for a landing. A freighter is making its way to Tunis, which is barely visible in the early morning mist. The Mediterranean stretches out broken only by a shimmering patch as the sun attempts to break through the clouds. Across the sea, the beautifully-shaped Bou Kornine, double-horned mountains described by Homer, dominates the peninsula of Cap Bon. Unfortunately, this peninsula is a grim reminder of the end of the Axis control in the last war. The Punic Port lies below and I revel letting my imagination run wild.

The Carthaginian empire had encompassed half of the known world, sending ships as far as Britain and Senegal. It was the home of Hannibal, Caesar, Hadrian, St. Augustine, Belisarius. Hamilcar and his son Hannibal sailed from this port, pitting themselves against Rome, Sicily, Spain and Portugal. In 146 A.D. Byrsa Hill fell to the Romans, and Carthage was completely razed and the soil sown with salt. Adjacent to Carthage is the suburb of Salambo where one finds the Tanit Cemetery with evidences of child sacrifices of Baal worshippers. Ports of Salambo and LeKram were headquarters of the Barbary pirates.

The aspirations, the unfullilled dreams, the humanitarian, the brutal; the hopes and the memoirs; vested interests and assistance programs; the Apollo, the riots—the melange of human relations in every generation; the ebb and flow of history—how fascinating; how challenging it all is!

This morning, the Punic Port lies peaceful and picturesque like an artificial lake. The sun, now bright, bathes the quiet suburbs of neat white houses with blue-trimmed windows and shutters. The varied mosques raise their minarets skyward. Behind me is the huge St. Cyprian Cathedral, now closed but housing the National Museum and the mosaic school. Moslems praying are not in evidence as in Jordan and in Guinea. The

Catholic Church is banned; Protestant work scrutably restricted, and one wonders what is replacing the vacuum.

We have enjoyed our two years stay in this fascinating and magnificent country of contrast: Tunisian robes and miniskirts; sports cars and donkeys; TV and no plumbling; the stretches of beaches and deserts; discotheques and the Ramadan fast; the boutiques, and the Casbah; Hilton Hotel and mudbrick houses.

School Board, French camp for Kent, Bill's work trips around Tunisia, Committee on Tunisian Enrichment Program for American children, the Blind School, Rome, and children's humor make up another chapter.

On the 13th we share with our friends our slides of the Holy Land, "Walking in His Steps." Margo arrives home from Rome on the 20th; Christmas at home. On the 28th we leave for a family holiday for a week in Germany before Margo returns to Rome, and we go on to Vientiene, Laos. After eight years in the Near East-Afro area, the cultural change should prove another challenge. Bill returns to rice reclamation work in the tropics.

Our thoughts are with each of you and it was a joy to have spent this precious moment with you.

"Faith does not come from wishing, but by prayer and by believing." This was quoted to us by our six-year old after Vice President Humphrey's speech in Tunis. It is something frightening to know what children retain. *Joyeux Noël!*

Vientiane, Laos
Christmas, 1969

The monsoons have stopped and it is now cool and comfortable enough to enjoy our screened porch. We have been through another eventful year while we contemplate our experiences, sitting here listening to the clip, clip, clip of the gardener's shears as he trims the lawn, the soft tinkling of the small bronze Kamakura bell from Japan, and the maid's crooning of a Thai song as she irons. Over in the corner, Bill's rock tumbler churns away, polishing some of the attractive Mekong River stones. This is winter, but frangipani, bougainvillea, poinsettias, hibiscus, and wild gardenias are in full bloom. Anyday some of the orchids Bill has collected from up-country will burst in color; the cattaleyas, the spray orchids, tiger orchids, etc, which Bill has used to decorate one wall of our house. Beyond our back fence is the jungle, and in the clearings are scattered tiny rice paddies and water buffalos, huts built on stilts, many with mere woven mats for walls. This culture of total naivete can only leave the Westerner bewildered.

Amid the aura of tranquility, one is ever aware that all is not well with Laos. There are check points a few miles out of town beyond which families cannot go without permits, Lao fighters zoom East and South, soldiers—royalists as well as Pathet Lao (communists) are about; we ladle soup to an ever increasing number of casualties at the Army Hospital and are horrified to find they are in their early teens but appear like old men; more and more Meo tribesmen from the mountain regions of the North and other refugees can be seen. We join the diplomats and experts in seeking some feasible solution to the problem of how Laos can extricate herself out of this impasse of twenty some years—embroilment in this confounding politics of neutralization. It is with mixed feelings that we write you this year. Nonetheless, despite our frustrations, our hearts go out to this land locked country.

Someday we hope we can really come to know the Laotians, climb the mountains, and poke around the hundreds of man-size stone hewn jar that sit immobile and mute, refusing disclosure of origin or purpose. They are probably the only remaining witnesses to the countless skirmishes and battles that have taken place on the Plain of Jars from the dawn of history of this "Kingdom of the Million Elephants." They know only too well that history repeats itself, as the plains once again are

34

the stage of conflict. We miss the sea, the souks, the sightseeing trips, but we have the famous Morning Market where every kind of food from beetles, grubs, frogs rats, exotic fruits, and fresh vegetables to jewelry, teak carvings, toothpaste, clothing, and pot can be found.

This is Saturday. Christmas rehearsals for the Sunday School program are over and as usual all activities emanate from the front door. Mark's teenage friends go directly to the refrigerator for cakes, cokes and unique Dagwood sandwiches. The Hi-Fi is next, need I say, anything about volume? They don't loiter long, for it's tennis, football, volleyball, or soccer. This is Mark's first opportunity to participate in organized sports and he's thriving on it—5′ 9″ to be exact. Kent's friends are busy rehearsing for their magician's show scheduled for Monday afternoon; admission, a penny. The days are too short for them with model and kite making, transitor kits, experimenting with chemistry sets and myriads of other activities. Kevin and his friend have built an ingenious irrigation system using linings from banana tree trunks. They just left with their nets to catch butterflies for his mounted collections or to fish for his new aquarium. This is our first experience living in an American compound, but the children love having so many friends. Of course, we miss Margo very much, as she is attending Mid-Pacific Institute in Honolulu. Her letters have been fewer but indicate happiness and contentment. No doubt co-education and senior year have something to do with it. Christmas won't be the same without her this year.

In spite of the severe travel restrictions, Bill seems to enjoy his work, primarily in the program to try to increase food production by double cropping during the dry season. This entails the planning, design, and construction of various irrigation projects and he hops about in planes and helicopters. It is a slow and sometimes discouraging process, but the signs of progress are slowly emerging. Sometimes we are too impatient to see the changes that are taking place at an amazing (relatively speaking) pace in this primarily agrarian country of subsistence agriculture. As Dr. Thomas Dooley said when he was criticized for using 18th century methods, "this is where we must start, but the 18th century methods are augmented by 20th century experience." Perhaps, we are trying to leap from the hand spading age to the electronic age without the intermediate steps that make this change practical. Although Bill's work is a far cry from the hundreds of thousands of acres of irrigation in the Columbia Basin or the 100,000 acres of irrigation systems that he constructed in the Jordan Valley, the 500 acre projects that he helps construct in Laos, undoubtedly, have as much or more impact on the economy of this country.

This year was a year of travel. We left Tunisia soon after Christmas and spent an exhilarating week skiing in Garmisch, Germany. In June Margo joined us from Rome and we departed for 2 1/2 months of home leave. We stopped in fabulous Hong Kong and visited rooftop schools in the slum areas, witnessed overwhelming poverty in the villages; visited relatives in Seattle; froze in Yellowstone, and relished the rugged Tetons. We reveled at the three family reunion in upper Wisconsin, and the Bayou country in Louisiana with Amy's southern hospitality. We were impressed with the personally conducted tour of NASA by Mr. Dawn, head of research on clothing for the astronauts. We spent a fun time with our very Texan relatives, and were invigorated with the mountain air and the majestic Rockies with the help of Alice and Albert. So it was on to Disneyland and Hollywood, and to beautiful Hawaii, where we reluctantly left Margo in order to arrive at Vientiane before school opened.

We cherished these moments of sharing with you during this season each year. We remember His greatest gift, sharing his Son, our Lord, whose teachings of 2,000 years still apply and more than ever must be applied in this year when man walked on the moon. *Happy New Year — Di Chai Pii Mai!*

Laos—One of Bill's projects.

Happy New Year to all of you. I vowed that I would not let this season pass without these precious moments to reach each of you. We cherish your friendships, love and concern. I drove out of the house at 6:30 a.m. to drive the 25 kilometers from Vientiane that we are permitted. With a full teaching load, three lively boys, church and community activities, I have missed the moments of solitude without the pressure of time and schedules. Anne Morrow Lindbergh writes: "...in order to think out my own particular pattern of living, my own individual balance of life, work and human relationship."

Except for a few taxis, ox-drawn carts and samlors (rikshas), the city is relatively serene and still quiet. The morning market was not yet bustling with customers, although the women had already found their places on their prescribed mats and were getting their produce ready for the daily on rush. With temperature down to 50 degrees, the people were clad in sweaters and jackets and seemed huddled closer to each other. This is winter, the morning air is nippy and often the dew, heavy.

The monks in the bright saffron robes were filing out of the Buddhist temples with their begging bowls. The young, thin boys most of them orphans and refugees who have no other place to go, never beg or say thank you. It is their privilege to collect and to share. The people are happy and eager to give of their own and this sharing is expected of them. Groups of families sat huddled around fires, warming their hands while preparing or waiting for their bowl of glutinous rice. There is no evidence of starvation, but malnutrition is common.

The motley young recruits were drilling at the army campgrounds and all I could do was to shake my head. We've been to the B52 Air Base in Thailand; we pass the Communst Headquarters daily; we are aware of the casualties; and we read about the attempted peace talks. In the streets, we cannot distinguish royalists from communists, but all are people seek-

38

Villagers working on a self-help project

ing for some measure of security and happiness, satisfied with so much less than we have.

Within minutes I am in the rural areas, along the rice paddies. I drove along the Mekong River and stopped at Thadua to watch the tiny crude boats plowing passengers across the river to Thailand. The time-old river, clear and sparkling from the Tibetan mountains; turbulent, cutting its way through gorges in China. The river this morning is placid and murky, continuing its way through the heart of Southeast Asia—life giving; life taking. Not long ago, we came at night to watch a festival. People lit candles on tiny floats and set them on the river. As far as we could see were lighted floats moving gently in groups. Though a simple ritual to cast their sins away, it attested to an admission of man's shortcomings and errors and the desire to relinquish them.

The social and political problems that surround us in Laos, that infuse the campuses in the states, and that erode the moral structure from the family to the family of nations, testify to the need for these admissions with a humble but fearless effort to reanalyze our values of life.

In June, Mary flew to Honolulu to attend Margo's graduation with honors from Mid-Pacific Institute. She wore the traditional holoku formal and was garlanded with beautiful leis. We stopped in at Expo 70 in Osaka, as I wanted Margo to experience something of the history and art of Kyoto and environs. She returned to Laos to mother the family while I remained in Tokyo to attend the National Science Foundation Institute.

Margo is now attending the University of Rochester and finding university life one of adjustments. Sports has been Mark's mainstay: captain of the Gold Team, lifeguard at the new Olympic-size pool, and swimming instructor for the Lao students from Von Dok Teacher's College. He received one of his first prize awards at a national meet. Kent is happiest when busiest and he's busiest all of the time. He went on a Boy Scout outing to Thailand with his dad. I had to scurry to neighbors while baking Christmas goodies, when I discovered he had used up my food coloring for his sophisticated pollution demonstration. Kevin has taken an active interest in Cub Scouting and remains creative, but continues with his philosophy, "I don't want to work too hard." We were a mother and son combination at the Christmas concert at the Ambassadors; he is in the children's choir and I with the Mekong Choralairs. The antiphonal singing of "While By My Sheep" was especially lovely.

In spite of the shrinking area of safe operations for Bill's work, in November he received AID's Meritorious Honor Award. "His high professional competence quickly won over the local Lao leaders who organized self-help volunteers to provide labor. He resolved a crisis by replacing rock filled wire cages with solid concrete dams. These structures represent a more substantial accomplishment than all the combined irrigation work done in the preceding three years." We have every reason to be proud of him. Although the military situation is rather "fluid," Bill's work is limited to "safe" areas and except for an occasional ambush in the "safe" areas, he says there is not much danger involved. He does, however, always carry a two-way radio wherever he goes.

One of the happiest moments this season was to sit and read your many notes. We rejoiced with you in your happiness and accomplishments, suffered with you in your tragedies, shared with you in your concerns. In closing, a simple cinquain (5,4,3,2,1 syllables) written in flight from Hong Kong to Tokyo:

> I watched the sunrise
> bathing through clouds,
> God's voice speaks,
> Would man,
> hear?

Happy New Year — di chai pii mai

Christmas — Rio De Janeiro — 1971

I've always kidded Bill about not ever getting an appointment to places like Paris or London. Bill was flat on his back at the hospital in Vientiane with his leg in traction when the impossible happened. A telegram arrived, *Assigned To Brazil, Rio De Janeiro!*

Bill left for the Latin metropolis in April. The family followed at the end of the school year, as Mark was very involved in his last year at Laos (soph) and I wanted to finish my teaching year. Our hearts went out to the Laotian friends and our Kim, struggling through the cvil war between the Nationalists and the Communists, each faction headed by a half-brother.

The children and I arrived in Rio last summer via New Delhi, the Taj Mahal and Lisbon. We really suffered from culture shock for months. What a contrast from the quiet, pastoral, spiritual atmosphere of Laos to a bustling, animated, and demonstrative culture of the Cariocans, as the Rio de Janeirans are called.

After witnessing a shoot-out experience from a Copacabana apartment, we moved into a beautiful Frank Lloyd Wright-like house in São Conrado. Water trickles down a living mountain rock wall in the vestibule of our house. We were fortunate to find this house. From high on a hill, we can see and hear the surf of the Atlantic, enjoy the large iridescent blue butterflies floating about, and across the street, the jungle with monkeys that scurry around.

The children all go to the very modern Escola Americana nearby, however, we drive through one of the worst favellas, slums, Rocinha to get to the school. Portuguese study consumes much of my time, quite a challenge from French. I volunteer twice a week at the school in the English Lab for foreign students. There are a few families scattered in this area from Bill's division for family activities. We are also getting involved in activities and visited the Methodist Povo de Providencia, wonderful Methodist settlement work carried on by a Rev. and Mrs. Way. They have pre-school/kindergarten, Bible, adult education, and vocational training. The project was built on the original port site to minister to the sailors and others in that district. I carried a little girl, who had been doused with kerosene. The parents couldn't light the match and the child, fortunately, came into the hands of POVO.

Rio claims one of the most marvelous, natural harbors of the world, truly "Cidade Maravillosa," Marvelous City. The mountains, beaches, lush greenery, tropical bougainvillea, hibiscus, bananas, avocado, and papaya are here for the picking. Diffenbachias, philodendrons, birds of paradise, and ginger all grow like weeds in the garden.

A car picks Bill up to take him to the office located on the 11th floor, overlooking Guanabara Bay. Bill's work has taken him all over Brazil but mainly into the Central/North portions. His main emphasis is on the integrated development of the irrigation, flood control, and power generation on the São Francisco River, which flows through the central highlands of Brazil.

Rio is known for its most spectacular accidents. The drivers, public and private, are wild; the temperament of the people, muy allegro; and Copacabana, a concrete forest, and beaches, seething humanity. There is so much to see and to learn.

The children have all started music lessons: flute, guitar, clarinet, and organ. Whoever comes home first on Tuesdays, gets his lessons first. The maestro, a bachelor, has dinner with us each Tuesday and sometimes we all have a jam session afterward. Really Great! Wouldn't you know Kent has organized a three member band and they practice here! Electric guitars and a drum!!! Kent was elected president of his class, Mark was snatched up by varsity football and baseball, Kevin is creative and his art pieces are displayed at the ceramic center in Copacabana. Margo is taking a semester off to work in Boston.

It is time to load the children and go down to the Union Churcn to help package toys and gifts, which will be distributed to the poor. Join us at the top of Corcovado and stand before the immense monument of Cristo Redentor, Christ the Redeemer, with his outstretched arms.

FELIZE NATAL

Rio de Janeiro, 1972

How I love this terrace on the second floor that spans the width of or lovely Brazilian home. Trees surround me on three sides; the woodland in front is a steep hill. There is the sound of the stream in front of the house. The sea, a short distance below, is silent in the calm of the morning. Marguerites, phlox, lemon lilies, geraniums, and marigolds are in full bloom, and we welcome the evanescent and coquettish hummingbirds that come for their nectar swinging in their feeders. Our three boys and Margo are still sound asleep, having worked together until midnight making all kinds of goodies. Bill returns tonight from one of his many trips to the São Francisco Project.

How I relish this moment of solitude with a feeling of contentment and heart full of thanksgiving. With Margo home, our presents are artistically packaged. This is the first morning when no one has commitments. The house is decorated, school responsibilities are over for the boys. There are 1200 packages for the lepers, 120 for a boy's orphanage, toys and playground equipment for another, shows, plays, programs—all completed.

The highlight of the season was the service of the fifty-voice youth choir called "What's It All About?" which we put on at our Union Church. It involved children, grades 1-12 in verse and choirs, solos, pantomine scenes of the Annunciation, and Mary Magdalene at the open tomb. The music was contemporary accompanied by Mark and Kent on the guitars. Kevin played the prelude, "When morning Hath Broken," on the clarinet. It was a most satisfying program. There was a message for all, and it was a very moving experience for participants as well as for listeners. It was based around the "Affirmation of Faith," using Biblical references from the youth translation "Reach Out."

Having survived the initial culture shock of a metropolitan way of life, we are well into the second year in this "Cidade Maravelosa." Mark is a senior, first string football, baseball

44

pitcher and enjoys the competitions with schools in São Paulo, Buenos Aires, and Lima, Peru. Kent is a photography bug, self-motivated in many interests and is president of the eighth grade. I can always depend on him for repairs around the house when dad is away. Kevin is still the delightful company around the house and loves to work with models, pottery, carving soapstones, etc. He has a swimming lesson at 9:30 in Mark's class. Three friends are giving swimming lessons this summer in the neighborhood pool. It is wonderful to have Margo home for the holidays to give us nippy discourses on Nixon and Vietnam; jolting ideas, nonetheless, wholesome with middle-age mastication. Margo transfers to California School of Arts and Crafts in Oakland on January 2. Being on her own for a year was a real education for her too.

Mary is relieved to have her Portuguese studies behind her and continues as Church School Superintendent, on the PTA and U.S. Government Wives' Board, serving as Social Service chairperson of the latter, and reading to the blind, etc. Bill's work has been very interesting but also frustrating. There is so much potential for development in Brazil with all the resources necessary for such development—the people, the land, the natural resources and most important of all, the financial resources. All Brazil lacks is the experience, not quality of technical know-how but quantity, from the actual farmer to the highest level of technicians at supervisory levels. Bill says, "Our job is cut out for us to assist Brazil to develop people with experience."

Our most delightful house guests of the year were eighty-young Mrs. J.N. Rodeheaver and my sister Mae. Mrs. Rodeheaver was inspirational speaker at the neighborhood Easter Sunrise Service, which was held in the garden of a Catholic Retreat Center overlooking the Atlantic. Yes, it was an ecumenical gathering and afterwards, we all had breakfast on our terrace.

We await a neighorhood potluck for Christmas, about 45, and there will be caroling, family skits, music, and dancing. Wish you could each join us. I've been longing for this moment

45

to visit with each of you. May His richest blessings abide with
you. I close with that thrilling song coming out of the hearts
of the young people:

"It only takes a spark to get a fire going,
And soon all those around can warm up in its glowing,
That's how it is with God's love,
Once you've experienced it,
The Lord of Love has come to me,
I want to pass it on."

Feliz Natal

Rio De Janeiro — 1973

With the heat wave upon us, it is difficult to realize that
Christmas is approaching. You may call us seasoned Cariocans
by now. After a very heavy schedule through July, this fall
there has been time for reading, Bible study, reflection and
reminiscing.

We recall the Christmas letters shared with you from the
Old City of Jerusalem, from tropical Guinea, from the Saharas
in Tunisia, from Byrsa Hill in Carthage, from the Mekong
River in Laos, and from the Cidade Maravillosa-Rio. Each
brings back memories, and yet the ways of men in the Middle
East, rule of suspicion and fear in Guinea, victims of the
innocents in southeast Asia, watchful waiting in Chile and
Argentina, the changing role of the U.S. in world affairs, the
demanding domestic changes growing out of Watergate, etc.
all leave us perplexed. The age-old question rises where do we
each fit into the pattern of the universe?

Heartaches caused by a will pitted against another, frustrations resulting from accommodations to temporary necessities,
dilemmas provoked by intransigence, distrust evoked by

machinations—all are experienced within families as well as among families of nations.

It is time once again to look upward into the outstretched arms of Christ, the Redeemer—a unique landmark here in Rio—to acknowledge the existence of a Being, who undergirds us with a sense of right, forgiveness, sensivitity, faith and love.

Much has happened again this year. In January, three families (16 strong, 3 teenagers) went on a one-week fun and hilarious bus and train trip to the tremendous and spectacular Iguaçu Falls, located at the Argentina, Paraguay and Brazilian borders. In March, Bill went to Vietnam on a month temporary duty for consultations on irrigation projects and returned with another citation from Washington.

Mark graduated in June and mom tagged along with him to Rippon College in Wisconsin, detouring at Lima to visit Cuzco and the incredible Machu Picchu, center and citadel of the Inca civilization. Wrapped in alpaca ponchos, we drank in that mountain air, surrounded by magnificent terraced mountainsides of the Andes. We marvelled at the man-made trapezoidal windows and blocks perfectly fitted together without mortar—all to honor the Sun, Moon and Mother Earth.

In Madison, Wisconsin, we gathered from Japan, Seattle, Texas, and Rio to bury our sister, who had been residing in Japan. Then two weeks in Berkeley with Margo. In between her art and studio classes, we scraped, scrubbed, painted her arty three-room apartment. It was so much fun to be with her. Kent is an electronic bug this year, and Kevin just returned from an exciting trip to Sao Paulo where he attended a four-day music clinic.

We're thankful for the many blessings, for families, for friendships of those who were here and now gone, the continued friendships through correspondence. May God bless you especially during this season. We shall be thinking of each of you as we put up our home-made figures for the Nativity scene upon the natural rock formation, which is one wall of our livingroom. The light casts a lovely silhouette against the white wall. *Feliz Natal*

Brasilia, Brazil — 1974

Brasilia, so vastly different from Rio, is man-conceived, man-inspired, man-constructed, man-centered. Despite its uniqueness and modernity, it conveys something of the artificial and superficial. The transplanted capital, away from Brazil's first love, beaches and mountains, is situated inland on a 4.000 ft. central plateau. The planned city rises and stretches out in the shape of a giant airplane, expressing man's indomitable will to conquer the interior of this vast hinterland of this tremendous country.

In its attempt to symbolize the 20th century, urban center efficiency, equality and oneness, the planners seem to have overlooked the vital aspects of humanness: originality and freedom. The Brazilian architect Niemeyer's style is contemporary—classical. He uses the media of concrete, steel, glass in harmony with water landscaping. The austere lines and curves of the Hall of Congress bespeak the future. However, these unique structures are all but dwarfed by the mushrooming Ministry buildings, offices spaces, aparment houses—all in the same ten story rectangular shape. Despite the wide boulevards, landscaped parks, clover leaves, the sameness of the highways, the sameness of the self-contained superquadras. The residential centers contain eight to twelve apartment buldings, mini shopping centers, neighborhood school. This sameness is one of the attributing factors to the unhappiness of its residents.

Little do the urban dwellers give thought to the miseries of some of the outlying satellite communities, the squalor of some of the unplanned cities farther away, harboring a populace that surpasses the population of the entire city itself.

We live in a house across the lagoa, but we miss the spaciousness of our Rio home. We will no doubt be heading that way during our vacation. We continue as a split family with Margo and Mark in colleges and the four of us in Brasilia. The second week after arrival in Brasilia, Mary started full time teaching at the Escola Americana: Sociology, Linguistic Approach to English, Asian Thoughts, Latin American History and 7th grade Potpourri elective. This is the day after school dismissed and I am hurriedly writing our Christmas letter.

Bill's work is also very different. With the phase down of USAID's operations in Brazil, he finds himself a chief of a tribe of two Indians, both competent Brazilian engineers: one in Recife, two and a half hours away by jet and one in Rio, one and a half hours away by jet. Very little of his time is devoted to his first love, irrigation and agricultural development. His work now consists mainly of monitoring the close-out of many projects. This means a full time office job PLUS the field monitoring, really two full time jobs. His area is roughly equivalent to everything west of the Mississippi. After June 1975, only he and one other will be left to cover an area almost equal to all of the U.S. He feels that the engineering aspects of the close-out can be finished by about June 1976. He is toying with the idea of staying on a few years in Brazil after the close-out, as he has had requests from many sources to continue his work here mainly in irrigation and agricultural development.

I close with a "Waka," Japanese poetry of 5,7,5,7,7 syllables, I wrote to challenge my students in Asian Thoughts. The result was six legal-size pages of Haikus and Wakas with which my students responded—sensitive, thought-provoking, and deep.

   Disinterested
Bored and insensitive youth,
Touches of love, deep,
Challenging, mocking, to tap
Wellspring of treasures unsaid

We showed our Holy Land slides the other night in a different place but the same story, which relates the life of Him whom we celebrate at this time of year. We extend our sincerest wishes and prayers to each of you and to tell you we cherish your friendships. *Feliz Natal, Abraços,*

Brasilia, Brazil — 1975

Another busy semester ended yesterday and we are frantically getting the house in order for the arrival on Monday of Margo, a recent graduate, and Kent, who has been staying with my brother's family in Madison, Wisconsin to try stateside school. His cousin will be coming with him. It will be an exciting Christmas. We shall miss Mark terribly, but he is working this year. Tuesday we take off for Rio to spend Christmas with our friends and then, friends all, continue south to Florinapolis to the shrimp and fish country.

We stopped there briefly last year when we drove south 2500 miles to enjoy the European influence and industry. We flew to Chile to spend New year's Eve and a day in Santiago and then to Buenos Aires and Montevideo. Five dollars for an ample steak dinner for three. (I ducked!) During Easter break, we drove the other 1600 miles north to Belém through the scrubland and included a visit into the jungle hinterland to a 25-year old Japanese community in the center of their pepper plantation and a short river trip up the Amazon.

Highlight, school wise, was the memorable High School Renaissance Fair last spring. They constructed two outdoor stages for four Shakespeare plays. My lot was Julius Ceasar. This fall the 7th grade Social Studies class presented Asia Night with exhibits, interviews, a Burmese shadow play, a Philippine stick dance—Tiniklin, a Japanese Bon Odori (dance), a Chinese Dragon Dance, and the lovely Laotian Baçi Ceremony of Love and Friendship. Simulations in Government class led to the capture of pushers and buyers and adult and juvenile trials. Legal hairsplitting sent us scurrying to find the Federal Narcotics Agent at the Embassy. U.S. History class digressed to convene as a constitutional convention to revise the constitution. They had a rough time trying to get five amendments ratified out of 15 proposals and 53 amendments. Sociology class tried to do one better than B.F. Skinner on a Utopian Experiment and simulated "Future Shock."

Bill, chief engineer for USAID, is left with a "tribe" of one chief and one Indian, a very capable Brazilian engineer, located in Rio, 800 miles away. Maintaining two offices in Brasilia and in Rio, Bill covers all of the engineering work left in Brazil, which included monitoring the construction of two hydroelectric power plants, one thermal electric plant (oil fired), approximately 200 schools, 12 wholesale market buildings, a mineral project, 5,000 kilometers of rural roads, several loans for purchase of highway equipment, and one urban sanitation loan. Despite his travels, he manages to get back to his lapidary hobby. His work with Brazilian emeralds and aquamarine is really professional now. Kevin was engrossed in his project "Hovercraft," which is completed but waiting for motors (4 months now). He is now engrossed in bottle cutting.

The world moves on and changes. The books on Southeast Asia we bought last year are obsolete today! With heavy hearts we cast our eyes toward the Middle East and Laos dear to us. Scientists today in brain research and manipulation have reached the same threshold that atomic physicists faced during World War II. With man's knowledge, he has the potent power, but does he have the insight of control? He can gaze into the abyss of destructon or into a horizon of concern and love. The difficult ethical and moral questions of society continue to haunt us.

Our annual Holy Land slide presentation of "Walking in His Steps" brings us back to the humble stable of Bethlehem. May His love bless and undergird each of us. Bill will be retiring from government service this June and Arizona is beckoning us. *Feliz Natal.*

Flagstaff, Arizona — 1976

We stood in awe at the Washington Monument and the Lincoln Memorial; the big cars zoomed by; in a stupor we walked up and down the aisles of the drugstore adjusting our gazes to the abundance of everything until we felt uncomfortable eyes behind us conjuring, "three experienced shoplifters!"

Four thousand miles we drove through "amber waves of grain," "purple mountains majesty," and "fruited plains." America! How good to be back. Phoenix was hotter than Hades and we fell in love with Flagstaff. We're settled in our home among mountains, pines trees, and unpolluted air. Skiing is just around the corner.

Bill enjoyed his four months of retirement, gardening, building shelves, China closets, and a stunning flower arrangement chest and stand that looks like something from Hong Kong. On November 1, he left for Shustar, Iran for his former employer Harza Engineering, International of Chicago on the Karun and Marun Projects. He is on the Iran side of the Fertile Crescent and is digging in the stamping grounds of Darius and Cyrus and the land of the ziggurats. He writes that there isn't a blade of grass, but that the water will be coming.

Kent and Kevin have designed and built a mode music module, and redid the downstairs family room with their concept of modern art, geometric surrealism and symbolism. A color organ mural is on the drafting table.

We left Brazil with many fond memories. The highlight was directing the "Saga of America," an extravaganza and pageant inspired by my U.S. History class. It grew to include a cast of 150 students in the Jr. and Sr. high school, verse and singing choirs, narrators, life-size sillouettes, a covered wagon, six feet rocket launch made by Kevin, Western shootout, Indian raids and dances, square dancing, the Charleston troupe, the landing on Normandy, Guadalcanal, Iwo Jima, and the moon landing. I finished the script during Christmas break. The theater in the round idea was used, except for the lifesize sillouettes which were on the stage. Highlights of

American history really came alive. It was truly an exhilarating experience, and we were very proud of the students, teachers and parents who helped as well as the talented art director. A Washington Monument was erected on the front lawn by the Pond. The pageant ended with, "The kaleidoscope of the news from the Middle East, Africa, Spain, and China looms before us, and the future unfolds and challenges all nations that happiness involves the dynamics based on mutual respect, shared resources, and genuine dialogues undergirded with spiritual concern.

For Thanksgiving we enjoyed being with friends from the Columbia Basin Project days and students from Nigeria, Thailand and Iran. Fall has slipped away with a course at the University, a Western Conference of Asian studies, and campaigning for an American Indian woman (she won). Carter will need all of our prayers, if he is going to do something about all he's promised. I am settling into church and school affairs, and there's time to "think out my own particular pattern of living and my own individual balance of life, work and human relationship."

Out of the school of prayer came, "Prayer is like a telephone; not good unless you use it; not too happy if all one way; if you don't answer, it will quit ringing...A redemptive person is one whose life makes every situation better because he or she is a part of that situation." Only with the love of the One for whom we celebrate this season, can we meet this kind of challenge.

Bill joins us in sending well wishes for the New Year. The welcome mat is out. Do come.

Flagstaff, 1977

"For Unto Us a Child is Born...And His name shall be called Wonderful, Counselor, the Mighty God, the Everlasting Father, the Prince of Peace." And so the 500 voices are rehearsing with the Flagstaff Symphony for the rendition of the Christmas story from the "Messiah." What a thrilling and exciting experience for all!

The city decorations and home preparations for the holiday season are overdue, but the important programs meet their schedules. The Advent Potluck at the church was a success, as we experimented with eight groups emphasizing, in preparation for Christmas, Intergenerational and interaction with fun. Each group took a different theme for thirty minutes and the presentations were unique and exciting. One example, from the Advent and Music group, a senior citizen and a pre-schooler on the xylophone accompanied the rest of the group, who sang and played other instruments. The children's program this year will feature St. Francis and his birds in a rendition of the "Carol of the Birds," Christmas in Old Russia, Luciadagenin Sweden, Lady Befana in Italy, Las Posadas in Mexico and will close with the children's pilgrimage to Bethlehem.

Bill arrived home in May in the wake of a snowstorm after six months in the deserts of Iran and just in time for Kent's graduation from high school. Kent has been really hitting the books at ASU in Tempe and loving it, and so has Bill, teaching part time in the Engineering Department at the university here, Mary's taking couple of courses and involved in substitute teaching. Being part-time Director of Religious Education, and writing the rough drafts as a legacy for our children out of our seventeen years' perigrinations, keep her occupied. Kevin covets his driver's license now and is dabbling in art, receiving honorable mentions on both of his paintings at the Arizona Art Festival.

Highlights of the year: an introduction to the delectable Bolita mushrooms of this area, speaking at the American

Graduate School of International Management in Phoenix, Bill on "Technological Transfer" and I on "Cultural Transfer, Spouse Issues," and an invitation to participate in the Arizona Humanities Conference in Phoenix with a talk on "The Woman and the Family."

Kent and Kevin had a preview of skiing in Colorado over Thanksgiving weekend, but are disheartened with the temperature in the 60's now. The mountains and ponderosa pines, the sparkling skies at night, and fresh air of Flagstaff are rarities. Come and have a sampling!

—TANKA—

Stars glisten; crisp air,
   in the solitude of night,
nocturnal artist
    brush paints frost on the rooftops
    man awakens and is stirred
      Joyous Christmas!

Flagstaff, Arizona — 1978

Christmas is tugging at our hems and we are behind, behind! Mary agreed to go back to teaching full time on October 5, which brought all kinds of new experiences. In addition to teaching three English classes, drama, and technical theater, she was the technical director for Rodgers and Hammerstein's "Carousel," a combined music and drama production by the two high schools. With the demanding schedules, manipulating ingenuities, and a tremendously talented cast, the two-night performance ended last night with capacity crowds that responded with fantastic enthusiasm. Bill and Kevin's engineering and artistic expertise were a tremendous boon to the technical crew. Wish you could have ridden on the colorful ten-feet diameter revolving carousel with six horses and viewed the 20 feet wide backdrop of a Maine seascape.

Bill was sent to Cape Verde Islands and to Tunisia for short-term consulting last spring and has been working with an Engineering Consulting firm here. Kent has made the dean's list at ASU in pre-engineering and continues to work part time with U.S. Geological Survey with whom he worked last summer. Kevin carried an interesting responsibility with the Coconino Mental Health Agency last summer. He just won first prize with his original World War II tank model and also received honors with distinction for his air-brush painting in the Central and Northern Arizona Student Art Exhibit. Margo was with us for Christmas, and Mark joined us last summer and caught 35 trout with his dad. Our year was saddened by the sudden death of my youngest brother, but his lovely wife and four beautiful children will give continuation to his life.

You must all come to visit Arizona and particularly this corner of the "Northland." The boys have gone skiing already. The Japanese garden we put in last summer is under a beautful blanket of snow. The group of 35 Japanese college students who were here for a seminar at the university, enjoyed a sushi party in our garden last summer.

Time is short and we want to thank you all for remembering us with your notes. How we love hearing from you. Our love goes out to each of you.

From Africa — 1979/80

Belated greetings and Happy New Year! You were very much in our minds as Bill and I spent a hectic but marvelous two weeks together in Africa. I arrived in Dakar, Senegal on December 21 with 369 passengers on a 747 Jumbo. Bill was at the airport at 6:30 a.m. but I was minus two suitcases. I had no change, but had wild blackberry jelly and relish made by special friends, a can of hot jalapeno chilis, two packages of Japanese mochi (rice dumplings), a box of chocolate nuts, a bottle of pickled ginger, two packages of Wisconsin cheese, and two delicious apples—all of which Bill dearly loves plus a special birthday cake, decorated with Flagstaff pine and cones.

The Lagon Deux Hotel with its orange, nautical decor, balcony that jutted out over the Atlantic, the pounding surf a la Rio de Janeiro were a delight. I was back in black Africa, the international crowd, French language, delightful tropical weather, red and mangenta bougainvilleas, palm trees, wide boulevards, modern buildings, the seedy back streets, the stench of sewage, garbage, and litter, the lame, the blind, and the beggars. There were men in smart European attires, and women in red-orange-green geometric and floral sarongs and sleeveless overblouses. Their heads were wrapped in gay scarves and some wore filmy and loose robes called boubous. Other men were attired in beige or white Moslem abayahs, decorated with embroideries. Mothers chatted happily with each other carrying their babies strapped to their backs and carrying trays of goods on ther heads, the tropical melons and French croissants all typified the mélange of Dakar.

A short ferry ride took us to the Isle of Gorée, an old fortress island, center of slave trade from the 1500's to the 1800's. We were with Alex Haley as he must have walked those same steps, corridors, and chambers while he ruminated over *Roots*. We read, "From this door, the slaves lose their names and become a number....This is the place of no return." Victor Hugo had written, "One human being does not have the right to own another human being." Holes were cut on the walls and under the steps for the wrists of the recalcitrants. The island's population is made up of 400 Moslems and 500 Christians. young, deft swimmers, dove for coins tossed from the ferry, while others skillfully maneuvered the windsurfs across the channel.

Two and a half days later, we left the luxury of Dakar, picked up the lost suitcases just before enplaning for the capital Praia in the Cape Verde Islands. I was on Bill's monthly circuit as engineer consultant for Cape Verde and Guineau-Bissau. Cape Verde (Green Cape) probably the most ill-fated of African nations struggles for survival against cruel odds. The archipelago is an extension of the Sahel; some children have never seen rain. The last sprinkling of precipitation on the Island of Sal was nine years ago; some islands have been without appreciable rainfall since the 1950's.

Cape Verde was a Portuguese colony until its independence in 1973, the destitute Republic struggles for livelihood, but the neat stuccoed villages, cobblestone roads and plazas are quaint, and the basalt rock houses are scattered over the hillsides lined with terraces built to catch any moisture, but the cornstalks were already curling. The mixed populations, predominantly Catholic, are fair-skinned and appear more European in culture.

As we sat down to dinner with the Consul and his wife, whom we had known in Brazil, we were to relive those overseas days—the power went out, they had had water two hours a day for weeks and the bugs bombarded us. The Chargé d'Affaire nonchalantly scooped one diver out of his goblet, never missing a word in his conversation—a telltale manifestation of a well-seasoned diplomat from the tropics. I later confessed to Bill I didn't know whether I could go back to the flying cockroaches, lizards, etc.

Our Christmas dinner, in the one cafe in the village of Tarrafal, where Bill has a school being built, consisted of a scrawny chicken, cooked over charcoal on a not-too clean oil drum in the patio, French fries and rice. Vegetables are a scarcity. The exhilarating swim in the turquoise waters of the

Atlantic and a hike up the side of a mountain compensated for the void in gourmet. The three-hour drive over cobblestone roads in the landrover would have mixed turkey and dressing or emaciated fowl into a similar substance. We enjoyed picking up hitch-hikers on their way to the well and passed out candies that Bill always kept in the car.

A unique trip by landrover on the Isle of Fogo (Fire) took us up to 6,500 ft. altitude and a drive into the crater of a volcano, where we saw farms along the edges, isolated villages, and lava houses built right on the remains of a lava flow. A moonscape, volcanoes within volcanoes, what could Walt Disney do with the jagged pinnacles of lava, or the undulating humps of serpentine formations? We were mindful of the heartbeats in its subterranean caverns. When we got to the backside of one of the volcanoes, I spotted a whiff of smoke and was convinced it was time to go, but the villagers assured us that the volcano gives them 15 day's warning, so that they have time to pack up their belongings on burros and walk out of the crater. The volcano has had 29 eruptions since the 1400's when the first Portuguese sailing vessels slid into the uninhabited islands. The last eruption was in 1951 and I was not about to give a blow by blow description of the next one.

On our descent we visited a magnificent German experimental farm. What a little water could yield from these parched lands! However, the expense of pumping water from sea level wells to these terraces does not pay for the production.

On to Sal Island (Salt), the most desolate and bleak of the chain, but it boasts a sophisticated runway and airport that lands the South African 747's and a Russian Aeroflot. These facilities were built by the U.S. Air Force for the WWII North African campaign.

We were up at 4:30 to catch the TAP plane. A 24-hr strike had been resolved at midnight and we made it to Guineau-Bissau, where we were able to unpack, take long showers, wash clothes, and cook our own meals in Bill's apartment. Unfortunately, the ferry was not running nor could we charter a plane to the island of Bolama, where Bill's main school constructon program was in progress. I really wanted to see this, the concrete block plant in operation, and the experimentations with solar water heating. With the cache of dried and canned goods in my suitcase and fresh shrimps, bought at the door, we were able to have a Japanese open house on New Years. Mind you, we had hand-carried turnips and tiny carrots from Cape Verde. The ambassador and his wife, 25 people in all, came and Bill was happy to be able to reciprocate their hospitality in a small way.

Although the pace was fast, we were able to enjoy our togetherness, walks, talks, siestas, and to participate in "bargaining gymnastics" in between Bill's office calls and business. It was a great 32nd anniversary honeymoon. Our best wishes go out to you and our prayers for mankind for the 1980's that rumble with hostages, Afghanistan, oil, violent crimes, and elections. How nice to have been able to walk the streets of these African countries with no fear at night. His promise:

"Ask, and you will be given what you ask for. Seek, and you will find. Knock, and the door will be opened." Matt. 7:7.

Flagstaff — 1980

It is almost warm enough to sit out on the terrace to write our annual letter. Conversation around the Thanksgiving dinner table with an Uruguaya, Brazilian, world traveller, and our children ranged from the hostages, energy crisis, Gang of Four, communication, education, earthquake, and inflation to Washington. So much suggested the negative; and yet, it was warming to start listing our endless thanksgivings and above all to have someone to thank.

Another year of highlights, never-to-be-forgotten trip at my sister's invitation through Middle Europe, including Budapest,

60

culminating in the magnificent and awe inspiring drama and music of Christ's story at Oberammagau in the beautiful Bavarian Alps. What a message the villagers have portrayed each decade ever sine they vowed to this presentation since this little hamlet was spared from the terrible plague of the 1630's. Our trip was like a panoramic review into the great historical struggle of our faith that surged through the reformation centers of Europe and into England and Scotland. The talks at the Women's Retreat last fall evolved into the theme, "I Believe in a Beautiful Faith," a "Courageous Faith," and a "Satisfying Faith."

Bill was able to meet us in London to do the British Isles trip with us. He was particularly impressed with the bonnie banks of Loch Lomond and the leviathan haunts of Loch Nesse. We are particularly indebted to our dear friends at Banbury (home of ride a cock horse to Banbury town) when Bill had a severe virus attack.

This is Bill's second year of work in Guinea-Bisssau and the Cape Verde Islands in the construction of inexpensive but utilitarian rural schools on the numerous poverty stricken islands. He is particularly enjoying experimenting with solar water heating and methane energy. He writes of his long trek "up into the 'city of clouds,' lost in the mist except for the sounds of crowing roosters in the distance." The intermittent glimpses of the valley below suggest an earlier era of rain that had given the islands its name 'Cape Verde,' the green cape. Today in sharp contrast, the islands are only an extension of the Sahel where many ten and eleven year olds have never experienced the delight of rain, and I am overcome with a sense of urgency and a feeling of purpose in the struggle for existence of a people overtaken by circumstances beyond their control..."

We look forward to a joyous holiday with the gathering of the family from Africa, Wisconsin, San Francisco, and Tempe. Kent was invited into Tau Beta Pi, which was denied to his father due to discrimination, and Nu Kappa Phi honoraries and will be graduating in early summer. Kevin loves his ar-

61

chitectural design courses and Mary is in her third year of teaching in Flagstaff.

Our prayers are with you in your sorrows and pain, our congratulations in your joys and accomplishments, our thankfulness for you for the sense of belonging and oneness through His care, love, and direction.

Santo Domingo, Dominican Republic — 1981

Greetings from Santo Domingo, Caribbean city of the conquistadores, the gateway to Hispaniola and to the Western Hemisphere. Last night we had dinner in the old Colonial City at a little sidewalk cafe, adjacent to the historic Gothic Cathedral of Santa Maria, which reputedly contains the tomb of Christopher Columbus. We tried to detect the pulse of life that throbbed almost 500 years ago and still echo through the wide plaza, the vestibules, corridors, courtyards, and the cobblestone streets, lined with palaces with distinct Moorish influence. There are homes embellished with grilled balconies, buildings with stained glass windows, or ornate coat of arms of Emperor Carlos I of Spain, sculptured from limestone.

Here walked Columbus, Ponce de Leon, Pizarro and others, who each played his role on the stage of colonial history. The conquistadores and settlers lived, wrote, loved and plotted; planned expeditions, drew up petitions and edicts, promulgated justice or injustice. The Spanish galleons plowed up the River Ozama, where the eager passengers with dreams or those who came without choice disembarked. The sailing vessels unloaded the regal riches, carved cornices, blue damasks, and crystal chandeliers during the heyday of the Spanish crown. Other vessels unloaded the remains, or leftovers of humanity, of man's cruelty. Once again we ruminate over the destiny of man. What is ephemeral? What is legacy?

Kent graduated *magna cum laude* and is now working as associate engineer for Boeing in Seattle. Kevin is in his third year in architecture and enjoyed working for his architect uncle in Madison, Wisconsin last summer. As for Bill, "Work looked challenging and is still so, but practically nothing can be accomplished because the government agency will not or cannot support the project—no personnel, no equipment, no supplies, and no transportation. I have never experienced such indifference to the implementation of a project."

Mary was initiated into Phi Delta Kappa educational fraternity last spring and is trying to live up to her promise by teaching 7-12 grade English in a new American School, which opened in September. We are undergoing many adjustments and frustrations, but are looking forward to Kent and Kevin's arrival for Christmas. We anticipate other family and friends to visit us in the Caribee.

"Gloria In Excelsis Deo," we sing this year in Spanish, Chinese, and English, a wonderful mixed congregation at church. *Feliz Navidad!*

Santo Domingo, Dominican Republic — 1982

Two dark green shafts of light pierce like arrows out of the sea towards heaven in the early dawn. We are on the balcony of a hotel in Barahona in western Dominican Republic and are awed by the phenomena that slowly dissipates into the pink, blue and grey wisps of clouds. The islands, only a hundred yards off shore, cast mysterious black shadows on the wrinkled Caribbean. A lone fisherman deftly casts his fish net from his tiny craft. With a lobster cage poised on the prow, a boat with three fishermen slips out of the shadows of the island and heads for the fishing grounds. Throughout the world, fishermen, who imbibe the morning beauty and serenity, must share a kinship.

The whole horizon transforms into pinkish and orange hues. On the left, a cluster of clouds has formed and climbs like the red cliffs of Arizona's Monument Valley, while on the right the great Thai Buddha lies with folded hands in prayer. Brush in hand, the artist has added tinges of blue-lavender to the clouds. Barely touching the water, a solitary crane has broken into majestic flight; another joins him, and yet another. In the foreground, our eyes follow the curved trunk of a coconut palm to the top, which is draped in graceful green-black fronds. The first rays from the rising sun stealthily creep through the trees changing the silhouette to dark green and the water to blue-grey. Morning has truly broken! Gloria!

Monument Valley is no longer. In its place is a concave bowl in gold, yellow, and orange; slowly and steadily it transforms into—is it a mushroom cloud? The phenomena of the greenshafts, the illusion of the mushroom clouds shatter us and we know all is not well; the enigma of peace and nightmare.

Bill has been faced with the redesigning of the irrigation system that was supposed to have been completed before his arrival on the project. Affected by the adverse economic conditions, the high fuel and low sugar prices, and compounded by the economic slowdown in the world, the contribution efforts have been frustrated, but Bill believes that there is still hope for resolutions. For diversion, he has added scuba diving to his hobbies, but has, as yet, time for only a few attempts.

Mary continues working with young minds; stimulated, frustrated, but ever hopeful, she tries to teach beyond book learning to inculcate principles and ideas to help equip them for lives of tremendous odds and challenges. A high point was the dramatic presentation of the "Highlights from Shakespeare" by four of her English classes last June. What an exciting way to teach the insights of Shakespeare to naturally dramatic young people. Summer visits with children were great.

We are looking forward to some of our family to be with us for the holidays; Kevin, Arizona State University; Kent,

Seattle; Mark, Madison, Wisconsin, and Margo, San Francisco.

Particularly at this time of year, we enjoy hearing from all of you and to visit with each of you. Your contacts mean a lot to us.

Confronted with the enigma of *Peace* and *Nightmare*, we must strive for *Peace* in our time and be able to sing the carol of the angels...

> Above its sad and lonely plain,
> They bend on hovering wings,
> And ever o'er its Babel sounds,
> The blessed angels sing.
> God bless you and keep you.
> *!!!Feliz Navidad!!!*

Santo Domingo, Dominican Republic — 1983

Clouds move quickly across the skies, transforming the blue into a sea of gray and black. A splatter of light rain is followed by strumming strains as they hit the metal awning of the terrace of our apartment. Abruptly the strumming sounds become a loud drumming and I am intrigued by the waterfull cascading from the awning and I watch "God Wash the World."

The brief shower stills the dust and fumes of the city. Now the spattering drops are coquettish steps on the puddles on the red tile floor. The rain is a sonata, moving from adagio to allegro, crescendos, cadenzas, and finally to intermittent plucking of strings. The tropical concert ends and yet every leaf of the mango tree, each palm frond, each rose petal, every branch of the bougainvillea, flamboyant, and bread fruit has been washed refreshed. The world yearns for these moments of cleansing its ever-increasing stains from the uncertainties in politics, economics, personal life and certainties of poverty, oppression, corruption, and self-righteousness. The brightness of the sun pushes aside the greyness and islands of blue begin to emerge. Upturned leaves of the canas harbor isolated pearls of water that now glisten like finest diamonds.

Another year has passed, a smorgasbord of happiness, contentment, anxious moments over a car accident and Bill's gall bladder surgery. A friend and he, both lapidarists, had the same operation within a few weeks and we kidded them about going into their own specialized stone productions. We enjoyed precious and happy diversions with our sons at Christmas time, and at school two of us co-directed "West Side Story" with a cast largely of very talented New York Dominican students. At one of the rehearsals, the rumble scene jettisoned into New York action much too realistic. The drama was presented at the American Dominican Center and proved a terrific success. A thirteen year old girl with a God-given voice was a natural for Maria, but to find a male lead was not so easy. When we found out about one who loved to sing in the shower, he was the one.

In August Bill and I plunged into a never-to-be-forgotten student life at the University of Salamanca in Spain—el curso Español intensivo. Afterwards we explored through Segovia, Extremadura, Andalusian Seville, Cordoba, Granada, and Toledo. We stalked through ancient dreams, achievements, intrigues, atrocities, incredible engineering and architectural achievements, spiritual zeniths and nadirs, inquisitions, betrayals, and wealth and poverty. We see today familiar evidences and her recognizable overtones.

We need to take time to drink deep of the well of eternal spring. "Great is His faithfulness; His loving kindness begins afresh each day."

We're anxiously waiting for Margo's arrival for the holidays. Kevin, a Gold Key candidate, postponed graduation a year to intern with the Industrial Designer at Honeywell Corp. After two and a half years at Boeing, Kent and four associates have branched out on their own in electronics research—named Seattle Silicon. Mark still continues at the Garden in Madison, Wisconsin.

In the third year of Bill's contract, a ten-man commission, directly under the president, was created to facilitate administration, and construction finally got underway. The polemics over adherence to specifications and contract terms remain unresolved, and we eagerly look forward to life again in the states at the end of his contract next spring. *Feliz Navidad!*

Flagstaff Among The Pines — 1984

1984 was a travel year. We left the Dominican Republic at the end of February, enjoying a leisurely one week cruise on the Caribbean. A 21-day Eastern flight allowed us to stop to visit with family and friends on our way back to Arizona. In June we took a trip to the Northwest to attend Bill's 50th high school graduation reunion, where he was a celebrity. It was wonderful to re-establish ourselves in our home again after a busy summer remodeling and repairing, the fruits of handy Bill's labors.

Margo is now working at the State House in Boston and enjoyed electioneering for the victorious young representative and senator. Mark stays put in Madison. Kent is a principal in the newly-named Seattle Silicon Corp, which is thriving, and Kevin after a year with Honeywell as a trainee, will be graduating from ASU in May. We have both jumped into church and civic activities and are finding out a computer is more than a toy.

We miss life Dominicana, but enjoy the fascinating crystal etchings on our windows in the mornings, and wish that we could share the magnificent snowfall, which, just now, is transforming the hillsides, pine forests and housetops into a virtual wonderland. Our sincerest season's Best Wishes to each of you, and we close on a serious thought written last July.

THE PLAIN OF JARS*

What havoc exploded?
Monstrous caverns like inverted volcanos
Gaping wounds, carved sinister grimaces,
Onslaughts of B52's bound for the Ho Chi Minh Trail.
The plane circles over hundreds of massive jars
Time and purpose lost in communal silence.

The plane lands. I face an awesome jar. He speaks:
Reverberations of the bombs still echo within.
I bear the wretched earth upon my shoulders,
See the bullet holes, the fissures of my torso?
Other jars join in antiphonal chorus;
I listened to the swishing robes of the enlightened.
I watched caravans of silk, tribute for palaces of Cathay.
I grieved for craftsmen of porcelain taken by the conquerors.

I felt the earth tremor with thundering hoofbeats,
Savage clashing of swords, Burmese and Thai.
I glimpsed a princess swaying in a golden palanquin,
A peace offering to the Kingdom of the Khmers.
I pled with the brothers, a nationalist, a communist
Charging their armies in bloody fratricide.

Avarice, jealousy, power, intrigue
We have witnessed all the base emotions of man,
Zooming planes, bursts of napalm, explosions of CBU's
Cries of anguish and terror of children,
Faltering weak, raspings of the dying.

Man who raised the temple towers,
Tamed the angry rushing waters,
Bridged the mountains, burrowed tunnels,
Painted treasures, wrote pages of wisdom,
Man who walked upon the moon
Split the atom, computerized chips.

*Located in Central Laos, close to Vietnam border.

Man endowed with supreme gifts of creation,
Made in the likeness of his Maker,
Why, O why are you once again?
Are MX missiles, chemicals, life but playthings?
Only you can will and change,
Wills into dialogues,
Swords into plowshares,
Holocaust into peace.

The jars fell silent.

Flagstaff, 1985

I am a silent witness to the masterpiece of the nocturnal artist, who paints a magnificent snowscape with deft fine strokes of diagonal lines, swirls of snowflake pointilism. The artist pauses as if to study her canvas and then resumes with hurried inspiration. The laden pine boughs, like string basses attuned to the full sweeps of aspens and cottonwoods, over the white strings play a symphonic rhapsody. Such experience is one of the delights of living at 7,000 feet.

What better mood for the Christmas season with its promise of Peace on Earth, ever elusive, but for which we all desperately seek.

And so our love go as to all of our families and friends at this yearly rendezvous. With heartfelt thanks we celebrated Thanskgiving yesterday, for our many blessings, health, family, friends, and work to do. Bill taught part-time in the Engineering Department of NAU last spring, and Mary is teaching the fall semester in the College of Education. Bill continues his many hobbies while Mary is involved with the United Methodist Women at the North district level, attended the regional school in Colorado and the national conference in N.Y., and enjoyed teaching the course "Native Ameicans" at the conference School on the campus here last July.

Kevin graduated, cum laude, in Industrial Design, is working at Harrington Medical Research Center in Phoenix, and is just starting a 3-month consulting job with Honeywell. We just visited Margo in Boston and Mark in Madison, and Kent is joining us for Christmas.

About a month ago, our family buried our brother Bob at Arlington National Cemetery. He had retired from the Fisheries Dept. Research at Smithsonian after many years. The brief ceremony with the honor guards, flag presentation, gun salute and the final taps, honoring him for his gallantry during WWII was moving. After the service, we stopped at John F. Kennedy's grave. The eternal flame and his ideals continued to burn. I turned to look for the well-known inscription on the stone wall. "Ask what you can do for your country." And so, ask not what church and God can do for us. Ask what we, together in the fellowship of all believers and concerned, can do for mankind, and God and His son who taught us the Way, the Truth and the Life.

Two poems were published this year:

ODE TO A BYZANTINE TEAR VASE

I hold you, tiny tear vase
Frosted, pale green, translucent
What hands, fire, breath molded you?

I caress your rounded body, slender sylvan neck
Like hands that held you long ago in Byzantium,
I see tears filling you with love, fear, loneliness.

Did your betrothed fight the raiding Goths?
Stumble to the Persians, lance the Seljuk Turks?
Carry to Jerusalem the victor's banner?
Or fall in the ill-fated First Crusade?

I would sing melodies, could you pluck your lyre,
I would rejoice jubilant, could you shout your ecstasies.
Tenderly I lift you to my china shelf
You to sit in beauty silent
I to muse in dreams evanescent.

MT. FUJI—Haiku and Tanka*

Red embers glowing
Twilight's flocculus spectrum
A cone looms majestic

Swinging lantern lights
Climb the winding sacred trail,
Hushed meditations
Join the spirit of pilgrims
Climbing Mt. Fuji at night

Zigzagged lightning flashes
A silver plane glides like a tern
Through thunderous clouds
Like Olympian gods, we
View awesome drama below

Five steps a struggle
Gasping for thin air, we stop
Around the bend come veterans,
The one-legged, maimed, blind cheer
"Take heart, on to the summit!"

The summit at last
Crater, gale, mist, and sunrise
Conquered and humbled.

* Haiku is typically a syllabic poem of three lines of five, seven and
five syllables. Tanka is five, seven, five, seven, seven. Haiku and
Tanka were popularized by Basho (1644-1694) through Zen Buddhism

Christmas Letter In Flight Over The United States — 1986

Totally in the hands of others, flying will always give me a sense of mystery and awe as well as time for reflections. Through scattered serrated clouds, I catch a last glimpse of ocean and skycrapers, and now valley and intermittent habitations.

New York was a sea of activity as new United Methodist Women Conference officers converged from all parts of the country to be oriented and challenged both in spirit and energy. The Statue of Liberty, Old North Church in Boston, Lexington, Concord, Middlesex, all spoke to me of heritage. The incongruity between heritage and recent scandals, especially in light of the upcoming bicentennial of our Constitution gives us much to ponder. The Administration's feeling of insulation and infallibility overwhelms us. Notwithstanding nuclear escalation, apartheid, hunger, atrocities, abuse, refugee problems, the greatest fear may be fear itself.

We are over Indiana and Ohio, and we fly over what appear like tundra and floating glaciers on blue water. In April, Bill went to Honduras on an irrigation consulting job just at the time of the Sandanista invasion! The State Department Seminar on world problems with emphasis on "terrorism" was an eye opener. Last summer we took an exhilarating RV trip into the Canadian Rockies with the Johnsons from Delaware. On to Vancouver and EXPO before helping Kent move into his new townhouse in Seattle.

Preoccupations in our own spheres of interests from which we can exchange new ideas, associations, and stimulations have been rewarding. An ambitious long-term planning for Kamp Kiwanis for the Handicapped, and a class on Church and Nuclear Arms were on the agenda for Bill; for Mary, UMW Executive Board Meetings, church commissions, AAUW, Arizona Advocates for Children's Child Watch, Hospital Auxiliary Board, and Poetry Club.

Cluster of shadows dot patchwork farmland over Nebraska and Kansas. I took advantage of N.Y. to spend a week with

Margo, who continues in Senator McGovern's Ways and Means Committee in Boston. I helped hang Margo's exquisite hand-made baubles on the tree, enjoyed the Nutcracker Suite Ballet, and the Harvard-Radcliff Symphony. Kent just returned from a business trip to Paris-Brussels-London. Kevin is busy building assistive device prototypes for Harrington and Mark continues with rare balance between work and sports, long-distance biking and tennis tournaments.

'Tis the season of the Manger scene in Bethlehem and Mary and Joseph, who knew the plight of the refugees. Peace, Love, humanity, Hope continue to speak to us.

The clouds are a regiment of giant caterpillars, accompanied by black shadows, that are moving doggedly, ever forward and onward. *Peace And Love.*

Flagstaff, 1987

We took a brisk walk yesterday, passing homes already decorated for Christmas. Luminarios lined the walks on the campus, the Messiah performances and children's choirs were thrilling. The joyous season is in the air, family reunions, celebration of His promise, but we are ever mindful of the growing poverty in our midst; the eruptions in Central America, Haiti, Philippines, Korea; hostages; economic turmoil; and the forthcoming summit talks. Nelson Mandela, imprisoned for more than 25 years and his wife Winnie, banished in her own country, continue to speak to the world as the most visible and articulate apartheid foes.

Bill is in Phoenix for two weeks for training and teaching tax volunteers for the elderly. His work on the Kiwanis Board, as the new president of AARP, the renovating our apartments in Cottonwood have consumed his time and energy. Mary's church and United Methodist Women's work at local, conference and regional levels keep her running. Pacific Regional School of Mission in Tacoma, Washington and the National Seminar in Columbus, Ohio, last summer made it possible to combine duties and vacation with families. The United Methodist Women's work keeps me abreast and involved in demanding global issues. Do we need a sabbatical from retirement?

We are grateful for continued good health, energy, and stimulations. Kent has taken a managerial position with UNISYS near San Diego and the youngest is in Industrial Design with Xerox in Fremont, California, so we look forward to spending part of the holidays with them. We are happy to report that Lt. Gilbert Kanazawa (nephew in Hawaii) received the Coast Guard Achievement Medal for superior performance on duty and that Cap. Tyle, Wash. D.C. (Gilbert's brother) was selected for Outstanding Young Man of America for 1987. We are proud of our young people as they will strive to find the balance between profesional expertise and creative community participation.

STAR GAZING AT THE PLANETARIUM

Last night I gazed at
      one nebulous galaxy
and saw one tiny planet
      embedded among myriads of
      heavenly bodies
I wondered at the precision of
      forces and movements
and dwelt on the magnitude of
      human crises

the fragility of this single planet
harboring its family of four billion,
      an awesome trust.
LOVE AND PEACE!

San Diego — 1988

"The fog comes on little cat feet"—Sandburg. Currents of early morning mists meander through hills and valleys of La Costa, California, giving an aura of the mysterious and the unknown. I stand on the balcony welcoming the morning fog.

It's been a restful Thanksgiving at Kent's condo after one of the busiest fall schedules. Mary, as vice-president of the Desert Southwest Conference United Methodist Women, Assistant Dean for the Pacific Regional School, elected member to the National Board of Church and Society and, finally, newly appointed member of the Scarritt-Bennett Board in Nashville. She has made weekend trips to Wash. D.C., N.Y., Nashville, Billings, and Phoenix—all squeezed in between teaching two English classes at Northern Arizona University.

Bill has just completed a successful presidency of the local AARP, is active in Kiwanis and AARP Boards, and continues with tax volunteers. As we meet we are able to support each other's efforts, the conversation and reports are always vigorous, exciting, and challenging. Bill has succumbed to one successful cataract surgery and will have the other eye done soon.

Kent loves San Diego and continues with UNISYS. Mark continues with increasing responsibility at Johannsen's Nursery, Kevin works under constant deadlines as an Industrial Designer and Margo has made the big move from Boston to Seattle after spending one month with each of her siblings and with us, giving her ample time to doff the Boston politics where she felt her creativity was being stymied.

We are all so thankful for good health, contacts with our children and other family members, and our many friends. This season we cherish.

The fog has lifted, the outline of white stucco houses and tile roofs, outline of trees on the top of distant hills, the lagoon and ocean beyond are all now distinguishable. May the lifting of the blurred and befogged scenery of a short time ago and now transformed into clarity of visibility bring us hope in the vital areas of the world.

The world watched with bated breath as the United States and the Soviets worked diligently to save a couple of whales trapped in the Arctic ice. Can we not extend the same kind of concern and sensitivity to those trapped in poverty, child abuse and loneliness; trapped as political prisoners and children of apartheid?

We anxiously look for rapprochments beyond Algiers, Glasnost, Santiago, Beijing and Seoul. The vague determinants that resulted in our elections leave many of us and the world baffled, and we can only hope for an administration determined to dialogue with the majority, congressional leaders to confront and address the vital domestic and global issues.

"There is a bottomless resourcefulness in each of us that ultimately enables us to transform the spear of frustration into a shaft of light."

—Howard Thurman.

Flagstaff, Arizona
Christmas, 1989

What exciting events are taking place today! People movements for democracy and liberalization in Eastern block countries, in South Africa, Cambodia, Vietnam, Korea, etc., but the racial tensions, drug violence in the United States and in Columbia, intransigance in the Middle East, Central America and China are disturbing.

41ST ANNIVERSARY—Snorkeling at Molokini, Maui and relaxing a la Hawaiian.

KANAZAWA FAMILY REUNION—the first week in July, YMCA Camp, Estes Park, Colorado remains a memorable family togetherness, especially for our professionally involved children in the fields of art, business, law, electronics, nursery, design, CAD architecture, computers, communication, research, management, and contracts. Tennis, volleyball, golf, skating, horseback riding, swimming and hiking—all in the mountain air.

SADDENED by the death of Mrs. J.N. Rodeheaver at 98, long-time family friend, who has meant so much to Mae and me. We lovingly called her our American mother.

BIGGEST CATCH—a 7 foot sailfish caught single handedly by Bill at La Paz, Mexico. What a thrill, but his arm was sore for three days running!

INVOLVEMENT—what opportunities are opened to all of us: Margo with Spectra Communication, Seattle; Mark—Johansen Nurseries, Madison; Kent, Manager of IC CAD Arch. with UNISYS, San Diego; Kevin, Indus. Designer for Tele Sensory Systems, Sunnyvale. AARP, Kiwanis Board, volunteer tax program, Girls' Ranch for Bill. He just returned from cutting 180 Christmas trees for a Kiwanis sale, the profits to be used for local social services. Mary will be Dean of Pacific Regional School in June at the University of San Diego, and continues with her conference, local church and Board work. Uppermost issues are Central America, Gospel: Media and Power, Galatians, U.N. Seminars in New York, Legislative Seminars in Washington, D.C., etc. I keep one class at NAU.

A few reflections from our wonderful family reunion:

HAIKU	FREE VERSE
a quiescent lake	cacaphony of laughter and conviviality
innuendos of twilight	percolating ideas and stategies
a stag statuesque	determination to challenge and to win
	hearty appetites and subtle humor
TANKA	indulging in the beauty of the milieu
songs of meadowlarks	creativity and sensitivity to others
brilliance of morning breaking	listening and giving
shimmering pine boughs	binding, bridging, building
blooms in mountain glen, meadow	springboard of
	the veritable family
	the ultimate
	the family of nations

—Estes Park, Colorado, July 1989

m a r i

Thailand — 1990

Sawadee from Hua Hin on the Gulf of Thailand, where we are unwinding after a three-week eventful *Kamikaze* trip through Japan and ten days in Thailand. Through wonderful missionaries and friends, we were able to retrace a great deal of the history of Christianity in Japan from the northern island of Hokkaido down to Nagasaki, stopping at major points in between. We were truly impressed with the dedication and commitment of today's missionaries, teachers, pastors, and social workers.

We visited numerous schools, churches, social agencies involved with minority problems, abuse, women, defense and peace; Christian Martyrs Memorial and Peace Parks in Nagasaki and Hiroshima. The two cities literally were raised out of the ashes of devastation we saw 43 years ago.

We were met and stayed with relatives in Nagasaki, Hiroshima, Oshima, and Tokyo; imbibed the beauty spots of famous Miyajima temple in Hiroshima and Koraku Koen in Okayama; visited the remains of 1500 A.D. Shirakawa village in the mountain of Gifu with friends; enjoyed the colorful 7-5-3 Children's festivals, and spent one night at our honeymoon Fujiya Hotel in the magnificent Hakone Mts.—all we could afford, The J Rail is an experience, racing at 135 m/hr and rushing through 36 miles of tunnel 800 feet below sea level between the islands of Hokkaido and Honshu.

We were treated to formal artistic kaisekizen dinner, eel domburis, seafood sushis, tasty hors d'oeuvres, and convivial shabu shabu fares in Japan, to succulent Thai dishes and exotic fruits, and loved the graceful traditional dances in Thailand.

It was a real joy to meet our 11-year old Niran, whom we've been supporting for 6 years in a village, one hour from Petchabun, and we were delighted to visit with his mother, a 39 yr. old widow in their home built on stilts with walls of woven bamboo. The children were delightful in the Child Care Center of Rural Community Development work under the Christian Children's Fund and the Government of Thailand.

The Asians are *Unruffled, Unspoiled, Untrammeled!!* We were impressed with the efficiency and courtesy of the Orient from the taxi drivers and enterprises, to educational and social institutions. We couldn't help but note the tremendous contrasts in cost of living over crowded Japan compared with plentiful land in Thailand; minimal tourists in Japan and tourist boom in Thailand; farmers threshing rice by machine in Japan and by hand in Thailand; the rural giving way to high rises, condominiums, shopping centers as commerce encroaches and the young respond to the lure of the city.

Hats off to taxi drivers in Japan and Bangkok, to Tuk Tuks (three-wheel motor taxis in Bangkok) to samlors (rikshas) in Hua Hin—all adroitly maneuver through mazes of traffic congestion. In Thailand, they cavort through crowded back streets, passing laundries, tailors, sewing centers, with people still working past 9:00 p.m. Along the streets, people are oblivious to the traffic barely missing them, as they are immersed in enviable conviviality over bowls of chicken curry or hot noodles or rice soups or playing peek-a-boo with a cute baby.

Thai markets—odors of spicy barbecued chicken; spring rolls; waffles wrapped around shredded sweetened coconut, meat and fishballs; soups flavored with lemon grass, scallions, and parsley; replete with Thai silk, baskets, name brand clothes, jeans, dried shrimps, squids, fish, and home industry craft items.

We have two days of swimming in the warm gulf waters, catamaran sailing, and we're pampered with orchids on our pillows nightly. We are enjoying this Land of Smiling People.

Bill is president of Kiwanis of Flagstaff and busy with the Volunteer Tax Program. In April, Mari was invited to go on a ten-day grass roots study tour to Honduras-Nicaragua and the team was invited to Violetta Chamorro's inauguration. Mari will be dean of United Methodist Women's Pacific Regional School at University of San Diego in June. She has just completed 3-year Regional and 4-year Desert Southwest Conference work but continues with Board work and local church commitments.

This season was highlighted with a birthday party sprung by our four children in San Diego. What a wonderful and special gathering of the family!

JAPANESE RYOKAN (Inn)
—outside Sapporo, Hokkaido, Japan

t a n k a

Warm tatami floors
open sliding paper doors
sound of rushing stream
curling foam round black rocks
painting frothy white crescents

h a i k u

Carpet of amber
auburn leaves spread on hillsides
washed with autumn rain

Naked silhouettes
skeleton trees shivering
in November gale

LOVE AND PEACE